devised and wrote The Blue Peter Book

60p

HELLO THERE!

Do you recognise any of these photographs? They've all been in Blue Peter. Turn to the end for the answers.

And welcome to our Tenth Blue Peter Book.

It brings our total of Blue Peter Publications to twenty-four—so if you've collected our ten Annuals, all the Mini Books, our Royal Safari, Limerick and Special Assignment books—to say nothing of our two colouring books, you'll have a whole shelf of Blue Peter!

1973 not only marks our tenth Blue Peter Book, we celebrated our one thousandth programme on February 15th, and what with the Blue Peter Special Assignments, Val's Roving Reports, the marvellous results of our Treasure Hunt for the Blue Peter Old People's Centre, to say nothing of winning two more top awards — the first from the TV Critic's Circle and the second from the *Sun* newspaper, whose readers voted us the Top Children's Programme for the fourth year in succession — we've had a particularly exciting year. We've had unusual expeditions at home and abroad, and we've investigated hundreds of years back into the past. Val crawled along a network of newly discovered sewers to find out about life during the Roman occupation of York, while

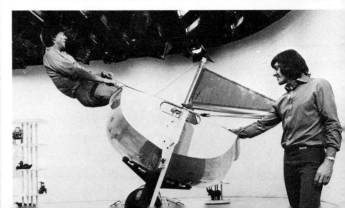

John flew to the northernmost tip of the British Isles to take part in the strange Viking ceremony of Up-Helly-Aa.

We've had a go at other people's jobs, too. Pete went mining for Cornish tin, Lesley put on a nurse's uniform and joined a class of trainees at St Bartholomew's Hospital, and we had a hair-raising time learning how to be speedway riders!

As well as getting out and about, we've had some interesting visitors who've come to see *us*. The Little Angels of Korea were the most colourful—we'd never seen anything quite like their dancing before. We met Mr Ray Cook of Pinner, who turns ordinary matchsticks into intricate carvings, and we were honoured by the visit of a real live Stone Age Chief, Chief Wamp Wan, MBE, from New Guinea who came to the studio dressed in his full ceremonial robes including a head-dress of bird of paradise feathers. There were many, many more and we only wish our book was ten times bigger so that we could write about them all.

That's what we like about Blue Peter—never knowing what's going to happen next—we hope you enjoy reading about some of our adventures in this book!

Valerie Singleton

John Noakes

Peter Purves   *Lesley Judd*

Petra   Jason   Shep

6

8

11

7

9

10

It's Lovely when you're in!

Every Christmas Day since 1864 the Serpentine Swimming Club has met in Hyde Park in London to hold a 100-yard race on the Serpentine lake. The prize is the Peter Pan Cup, originally presented to the club by the author J. M. Barry. A bronze statue of Peter Pan stands on the bank of the lake. But to the regular members of the club, Christmas Day is one of the warmer days, because they swim weekly straight through January and February when they sometimes have to break the ice before taking the plunge.

Why do they do it?

Some would say because they're brave, others because they're bonkers!

I went to join them in the comparative luxury of an early December day with the air temperature starting at 45°F. and the water temperature a mere 36°F.

You can join the club at any age. The youngest member is Sean Kelly who is 12, and the oldest is Sam Youlton who is 79. But there's a law which says "Ladies are not allowed to bathe in the Serpentine in the winter months". Lesley, who'd gone there with me, didn't seem upset by this at all.

"I'll tell you what, I'll stay on the bank in my big, stuffy coat, while you have your nice, refreshing swim. I might even make a cup of coffee ready for when you come out."

We all trooped out on the diving-board and stood a line abreast waiting for the starter. It was like facing a firing-squad; but there was no turning back now — the honour of Blue Peter was at stake.

It's a handicap race, each swimmer is given a number and you're not allowed to dive in till your number is called.

"Twenty-eight," called the starter, and 79-year-old Sam plunged into the water as though it was the Indian Ocean.

Then it came.

"Number 9."

I'd been dreading this moment for weeks, but when I hit the water it was ten times colder than my wildest imagining.

December in the Serpentine. Water temperature 36°F. Air 45°F. My skin — bright blue!

Warm towels gradually brought my circulation back.

The joy of putting my feet into hot water almost made up for the freezing swim.

Lesley made us all a mug of scalding coffee.

Old Sam was ploughing along beside me like a porpoise.

"Not so bad when you're in, is it?" he said.

"It'll be even better when I'm out," I thought, but I didn't say anything. I wasn't capable of speech.

Lesley was waiting on the bank with mugs of steaming coffee, and somebody produced a bath full of hot water. It was almost worth the whole experience just to put your feet into that bath — like stopping banging your head against a brick wall!

They presented me with a splendid badge, making me a member of the Serpentine Swimming Club, which meant I could enjoy a swim like this every week throughout the winter.

I thanked them all politely for their kind invitation, but somehow I don't think they'll be seeing too much of me in the future!

This badge entitles me to swim in the Serpentine all through the winter — should I fancy it!

7

If someone told you that a horde of prehistoric monsters had been spotted in Yorkshire and were heading for the Isle of Wight, I doubt if you'd believe it. But it did happen, and nobody panicked! These monsters were man-made, and getting them to their destination was a mammoth moving job. I went along to lend a hand.

MONSTER AIRLIFT

1 My first job was to help heave a Triceratops on to the waiting lorry. It was made here at this factory in Hunmanby and every detail was correct.

2 Looking at his giant teeth, it's odd to think that when he roamed the earth 70 million years ago, the Triceratops ate only plants.

3 The Triceratops was the first of a convoy of monsters to leave the factory. Others were to follow the same 260-mile route via Goole, Doncaster, the North Circular, Farnham, and the Isle of Wight ferry, to a new monster park at Blackgang Chine.

6 Monsters are an awkward shape when you try and string them up like parcels. I had to be careful not to break the spines of the Stegosaurus.

4 By the end of the week, Blackgang Chine was littered with monsters. The Triceratops had been joined by a Stegosaurus, a Brachiosaurus, a Polacanthus and then a Tyrannosaurus Rex. The problem now was to get them to their site at the bottom of a steep cliff.

5 The answer was a Westland Wessex helicopter piloted by Captain Yates. He said I could give Tony, the winchman, a hand.

7 Soon we were soaring over the Chine with a 40-foot monster swinging on the end of our hook. People looking up at the helicopter overhead were startled out of their wits!

Once installed in the park, the monsters looked great, just as they did millions of years ago as they tramped through primeval swamps and forests. Maybe it's as well that they died out when they did!

A birds eye view of Rome

SPECIAL ASSIGNMENT

As well as making films, we found time to take a few snapshots in the cities to keep for our own photograph albums. These are some of the pictures the "Blue Peter" film crew took of me.

Eating ice-cream by Rome's Trevi fountain

Exploring Montmartre, Paris

Relaxing by the River Seine with Notre Dame Cathedral in the background

London's famous Tower Bridge

With Kees de Roven on a canal in Amsterdam.

Place du Terte Montmarte

Sitting on a cannon ball at the Tower of London.

A rijstafel feast in one of Amsterdam's Indonesian resturants

Beneath the dome of St Paul's Cathedral

Edinburgh's monument to Sir Walter Scott.

By Strauss's grave in Vienna's Central Cemetry

Driving along Vienna's Ringstrasse

BLEEP AND BOOSTER

Bleep and Booster were furious when their favourite videoscope show, "The Scarlet Planet Avengers", was suddenly interrupted for a news flash. For a second the screen went blank and then the announcer appeared:

"Signals from the Planet Romanus indicate a serious situation . . ."

Bleep gave a great yawn.

"Tell me something new," he sighed. "There's always been trouble on Romanus! Let's switch it off and go and play suckerball."

"No, wait a sec," cried Booster, who'd been half listening. "I think something really has happened this time!"

The announcer carried on:

". . . Reports from the Planet Romanus indicate devastating crop failure. All Romanoids are starving. Urgent meetings at Miron HQ have resulted in a decision to meet the Romanoid request for Plantorisers . . ."

"Crumbs," said Bleep. "It must be important. Miron has never shared the secret of Plantorisers with any other planet."

Now the picture had changed to a group of men leaving Miron HQ and over it the voice announced:

"Leading the Peace Mission will be the Captain of the Space Commandos—"

"It's your Dad, Bleep," cried Booster. "Look, he's going to make a statement."

They leant forward eagerly to catch every word as the Captain walked towards a battery of microphones held out by a throng of newsmen. As the camera cut to a big close-up, the Captain's face looked very grave.

"Men of Miron," he said. "For thousands of years, the Romanoids have been our enemies. Now they come to us for help. If people are starving we must be merciful. Only our miracle quick-grow ray can save them. We shall go in peace, and in return for the food and prosperity our Plantorisers will provide, we shall ask the Romanoids for a Treaty of Perpetual Peace between our planets."

"A Peace Mission to Romanus," marvelled Bleep. "It's like a miracle!"

"And it will be your Dad that brings it off!" laughed Booster. "Let's ask if he can take us with him. I've always wanted to meet a Romanoid!"

Three weeks later both boys felt they never wanted to see a Romanoid again. The Captain had taken them to act as aide and secretary, and for twenty-one long days they'd stood and listened to a lot of boring talk between the diplomats, and they knew the Captain was having a difficult time.

"They're a nasty-looking lot, these Romanoids," thought Bleep as he looked round the conference room. "I don't like their horrid helmet heads, and their scarlet eyes give me the creeps. If I was the Captain, I wouldn't lift a finger to help them."

At that moment the Captain took the pen from Traitorus, the Romanoid leader, and with a flourish signed the Treaty of Friendship. Bleep looked on anxiously as with one stroke of his pen, his father ended centuries of non-stop warfare between Miron and the planet Romanus.

Bleep and Booster knew that they were witnessing an historic moment, but even though they'd been allowed to stay behind for the peace celebrations when other members of the mission had returned that morning to Miron, they weren't looking forward to them much. These Romanoids were a grim lot.

Suddenly, the tension in the conference room was shattered. Fido, Booster's little green space dog, had slipped from his coat and was grunting and growling under the table. Even the Romanoids laughed, but the Captain's strained nerves suddenly snapped.

"Get to your quarters," he barked to Bleep and Booster, "and take that yapping dog with you. You defied my orders in bringing it here. Now you can stay in your rooms and keep that dog with you until we leave for Miron."

Guiltily, Booster grabbed Fido, and he and Bleep slunk out of the room.

"Now you've done it," said Bleep. "Another dreary day here and not even the celebrations to pass the time." He was furious with Booster and slumped down on his bed. Then he relented.

"Here you are, Booster," he said, passing a tattered roll of Gamma Gumdrops. "There's only a couple left, but as soon as we're home, we'll get a refill." He made a quick count. "It's not so bad—one each and one for Fido!"

Booster laughed as he took the roll and picked one out for the little dog. But Fido didn't beg as usual. He already had a mouthful and was chewing away.

"Leave," cried Booster, and from Fido's mouth he took a chewed-up roll of paper. But as he started to read it, Booster got more and more puzzled.

"What do you make of it, Bleep?" he queried. "Just listen to this:

WONX NIAX TPAX CLLX IKX

Fido must have picked it up in the conference room. It's in Romanoid, but it might just as well be in Rubbish!"

But Bleep wasn't laughing. He grabbed the paper, and as he stared at it, his face went pale and his antennae drooped.

"It's as clear as your silly smug face," he snapped. "Read it backwards and leave out the Xs, and what do you get? KILL CAPTAIN NOW."

"The Romanoids double-crossed my father. Now they've got the Plantoriser formula and they're going to kill him." Green tears were already rolling down his cheeks.

"Pull yourself together," shouted Booster, "and follow me. We may not be too late to warn the Captain." Booster snatched up Fido and ran from the room, with Bleep following hard on his heels.

As they rounded the corner and ran to the main square, they stopped dead in their tracks. There was their space ship smashed to bits and the Captain, surrounded by a spear-thrusting mob of Romanoids who were prodding and shoving him towards a dark, prison-like building. Traitorus himself was egging his men on, and the Captain, unarmed as he was on this Peace Mission, was powerless to help himself.

Bleep and Booster watched, horrified. They, too, were unarmed. All they had on them were two Plantorisers, the symbols of peace.

At that moment, Traitorus spotted the boys as they cringed against the wall.

"Get them," he cried. "Those boys mustn't leave this planet alive. We have the secret of the Plantoriser and no one must return to Miron to tell of our treachery!"

Roughly the Romanoids flung the Captain into the building, slammed the door and then turned menacingly on Bleep and Booster.

Shocked by what they'd seen, Bleep and Booster didn't hang around. As one, they ignited their jet packs and took off over the walls towards the nearest cover.

13

As they landed they could see they'd touched down in a huge field of purple carrot-like vegetables, and they flung themselves headlong into them.

"They weren't short of food at all, Bleep," muttered Booster fiercely. "The whole thing was a trap."

"And we're caught in it," cried Bleep. "Look!"

Cautiously, the boys peered through the feathery leaves and saw the Romanoids lumbering across the plain towards them.

"They'll spot us in no time," said Booster. "There's no cover in a carrot. Better get ready for a fight."

Instinctively, the boys reached for their rayguns —then looked at each other in horror. In their hands each held only a little silver tube—a simple Plantoriser, which could harm no one. Already the Romanoids were on the edge of the field.

"If only we'd been allowed to bring rayguns," moaned Booster. "Now we're doomed."

"Not yet," cried Bleep. "There's still a chance." Quickly he aimed his Plantoriser at the stalks and fired. Instantly they thickened and grew. Now Booster was firing, too, and within seconds they were surrounded by an impenetrable purple wall.

"We've done it!" shouted Bleep, delightedly. "We've made an instant stockade. Nothing can get in here. Just listen to those stupid Romanoids trying to hack their way in! Aren't you pleased, Booster? Don't you think I'm clever?"

"No," said Booster grimly. "The Romanoids can't get in, but there's one thing you've forgotten. We can't get out!"

As night fell, the two boys huddled together in the darkness and whispered out a plan.

Outside they could hear the Romanoids snorting and grunting round their stockade. They had to work quietly and they had to work fast.

First they took off their jet packs. They knew they didn't carry enough fuel to get themselves back to Miron, but two packs might just be enough for one green dog.

"Lots of luck, Fido," whispered Booster as he slipped an SOS under his pet's harness and fastened the jet packs. "You've carried one

message for us today, let's see if you can manage another."

Fido's little yellow tongue licked Booster's hand. Then with one touch of the ignition control, Booster sent him rocketing off into the night. He could hardly bear to watch as his pet disappeared and he wondered if he would ever see him again. But the Captain had to be rescued somehow, so he turned away to help Bleep with the second part of the plan.

Bleep had been busy. He'd taken the topmost leaves of one carrot stalk and bent them back to the ground. Then he plantorised it.

"Help me tie it down, Booster," he gasped. "It's so tall and springy now I can hardly hold it."

Between them they tied down the leafy branches with the webbing from their belts. Next they both blasted it again with their Plantorisers, and immediately the stalk grew into a strong tree as powerful as steel. Then they clung to the branches and got out their pocket knives.

"Now," whispered Bleep.

One minute they were slashing at the webbing, and the next, the tree shot upright, catapulting the boys up and over the stockade, soaring through the air back to the Romanoid City.

They landed so heavily in a pile of sand that all the wind was knocked out of them. But they opened their eyes to a wonderful sight. There was the Captain standing before them, and quite alone.

"Father," cried Bleep. "They've let you go."

But Booster took one look at the Captain's sad face and realised the truth.

They'd landed in a vast stone walled arena, filled with a mob of Romanoids all screaming for their death. A dreadful fate lay in store for them all, for at the far end, cages of monsters were being wheeled in, all snarling and ready to kill.

"Goodbye, my boys," said the Captain, as they all clung together. "We must die bravely for the honour of Miron."

"Not yet," cried Booster. "We've still got Plantorisers. See those weeds growing between the stone blocks. Fire at them!"

As they blazed away, the weeds grew enormous. In an instant they were like giant trees whose roots and branches levered the stones aside like toy bricks. The devastation was terrible. Within seconds the walls crumbled and crashed, sending the Romanoids spinning to destruction. Traitorus was the first to go, but even now, a new terror threatened. A vast chunk of stone had split open the monsters' cages. They were lumbering towards Bleep and Booster over the rubble, with their long tongues outstretched.

"We can't plantorise them," wept Booster. "They'll get even stronger!" The boys stood rooted in terror as the slavering monsters advanced, with blood-curdling shrieks.

"There's one last chance," shouted the Captain, and he grabbed at one of the giant weeds and brandished it like a club.

As they felt the hot breath of the leading monster, the Captain smashed the club down on it with superhuman strength.

KERRUNCH! The huge jaws splintered the club as though it were a lolly stick, and the Mirons leapt for shelter behind a block of stone.

"It's all up, Father," moaned Bleep faintly.

"Goodbye, Booster," and he closed his eyes. At that instant engines whirred overhead.

Booster opened his eyes in astonishment as the sky suddenly blazed with light. In a flash, the arena was filled with the blistering white rays of destructor guns, and all around them the monsters lay in shrivelled lumps.

"We're saved," cried Booster. "It's the Space Commandos!" As the first spaceship landed, he saw to his delight a little ball of green fur come bounding out of the airlock and race towards him.

"It's Fido!" he cried. "He did get through."

Even the Captain gave the little dog a pat.

"I'll never send him away again," he laughed. "He saved my life, and yours, too, boys."

"I know," said Booster. "He may look a bit funny, but he's a real working dog and the best messenger in the Galaxy."

THE CORNISH ADVENTURE

A Cornish tin mine in the nineteenth century. Legend says the Cornish tin trade started more than two thousand years ago.

If you've ever holidayed in Cornwall, you'll be familiar with its magnificent coastline, with rocky cliffs and sandy coves. I used to think Cornwall was made for holidays, because of the marvellous sands for bathing, and the huge breakers for surfing, and the harbours for boating.

But when Pete and I went down with the "Blue Peter" cameras, we saw all over Cornwall strange buildings – tall brick and granite towers, rising up straight out of the earth, and pointing to the sky.

Sometimes we found them inland, gaunt against the skyline, and sometimes we saw them right on the cliffs, watch-towers looking out to sea.

I was told that they were not ancient castles – they had only been there for about a hundred and fifty years. They were the ruins of old tin mines.

I discovered that once Cornwall, the holiday county, was one of the great industrial centres of Britain. Pete and I decided to investigate.

Mixed with the earth and rocks of Cornwall, there are rich deposits of tin. Reaching this precious metal is far from easy, but for centuries the lure of this hidden wealth deep under the ground has had a strong pull on the Cornish people. For some it brought riches, for some it brought disaster, and for most it meant a lifetime of hard work.

Legend says the Cornish tin trade started more than two thousand years ago, long before the mine buildings existed. Some say the tiny island now called St Michael's Mount was the heart of it all, as merchants and traders came from the Mediterranean and North Africa, with

silver coins and jewels and rich materials. There, on the open beach, they exchanged them for Cornish tin. The traders mixed the tin with copper, and then they made weapons and shields and pots for cooking.

The Romans came here and wanted tin, too. They may even have brought slaves from their vast Empire to get it. On the mainland opposite St Michael's Mount, we saw a village called Marazion – some people say this strange name

Conditions were crude and dangerous, and the miners worked long hours.

17

"Candle hats" like this were the miners' only source of light.

Cornish miners at Redruth, June 1923.

Val as a bal maiden—one of the women who worked at the pit head.

means "the bitterness of Sion", and that it was called this by unhappy Jews brought by the Romans all the way from Jerusalem.

For centuries, though, men searching for tin only worked above ground. Tin was found up on the moors, in the streams among the gorse and heather. Tinners worked as they pleased, sorting out the valuable metal, leading solitary lives.

Eventually the tinners found that there was more tin underground than ever washed down the streams, so they began to dig pits to get at it. Then they dug shafts and passages.

Cornish tin mining—not just surface tinning—had begun.

Though going underground was profitable, it was crude and dangerous, but since the world was ready to buy up all the tin that Cornwall could produce, Cornishmen set out to invent ways and means of getting tin out of the ground more easily.

When a new mine was opened, it was a splendid occasion. Crowds gathered, flags flew, and the mine was named by breaking a bottle of port wine, rather like the launching of a ship.

The Cornish word for mine was Wheal, and the Cornish mines had wonderful names— Wheal Prosper, Wheal Busy, Wheal Friendly, Wheal Dream, and Wheal Mary Ann.

The engine house was the throbbing heart of the mine, and was the centre of a bustling scene. Next to the engine was the boiler house, then the Accounts Office, where all the business was done. There were stores for rope and tools, a "dry" where the miners hung their working clothes, stabling for horses, and great sheds where the ore was sorted after it had been crushed.

All the machinery and building was very expensive, and the miners could not buy it for themselves. Outsiders joined together with their money, hoping to make a profit—Adventurers, they were called.

Every three months, the Adventurers met together for an enormous meal. They ate beef, and loads of vegetables and giblet pie, Cornish cream and brandy punch. They were all served on plates and dishes made out of tin from their own mine. This was the Accounts Dinner, and afterwards they used to hear how much

profit the mine was making. The Adventurers got very rich.

But the miners, the men who worked below the surface, stayed poor.

Each day the miners gathered together by the engine house, calling to each other as the steel beam moved up and down against the sky, waiting for the bell to call their shift to work.

Every miner dressed in a thick red flannel shirt, canvas jacket and trousers stained with mud and clay, and heavy boots. He had a kind of skull cap on his head, and a hard hat. He used to stick a candle on his hat with a lump of clay, and then light it. There were no lights down the mine, and no poisonous gas problem, so the naked light was not a danger.

The mine captains, who were overseers, or foremen, used to wear tall top hats, and white drill coats.

Women worked for the mine too, never underground, but on the surface, sorting and carrying the crushed ore. They wore a heavy canvas apron over a thick skirt, and a big sunbonnet, called a gook, over the head and neck. Sometimes they tied their hair up in a

The miners were poorly paid—an average wage would be £3·00 a month.

18

coarse net called a snood. They were called "bal-maidens"–"bal" is another Cornish word for mine. Their work was very hard and heavy, and I thought the bal-maidens must have been very tough ladies indeed!

But conditions were even worse for the men who worked underground for eight hours at a time. It was desperately hot and wet, stagnant and unhealthy, and dangerous too, with risks of floods, and landslides. The miner rarely lived to be more than fifty.

He stayed poor. He was not paid regular wages, but "tribute"–so much for the tin he actually brought to the surface. It was generally about £3·00 a month.

The miner started young–often as young as nine or ten. Fathers would take their sons with them to work, and carry them on their backs when the long day's work was done, and the boys were too exhausted to climb up the rough wooden ladders to the surface–sometimes the ladders stretched up fifteen hundred feet to the cliffs above their heads. The mining engineers came up with an invention that did away with climbing all those ladders–a sort of lift, called a man-engine.

After the day's work, the miners all tramped home along the lanes; sometimes they had to go as much as five or six miles from the mine. Mostly they walked; the few lucky ones had donkeys, and were very proud of them.

When they got home, their supper was often only potatoes, or porridge–there were no great Accounts Dinners for the miners.

The life of the whole community, men, women and children, lay between the mine and the village, with its cluster of grey cottages and its barn-like chapel.

The Cornish miner was a sturdy, determined man, taking his hard life for granted. "A tinner's never broke till his neck's broke," an old saying claimed.

In those days there were three hundred mines in Cornwall, employing a hundred thousand people. Cornwall provided more than one half of the tin supply of the whole world.

Then, about eighty years ago, tin was discovered in Australia and Malaya, where production costs were cheaper than in Cornwall. One by one, Cornish mines, all but a handful, closed down. Miners were out of work. Many of them went overseas, taking their skills with them. Their villages became deserted, the paths overgrown, and the lifeless empty cottages fell down.

Ivy crept over the old engine houses and brambles covered the deep shafts. Silence fell over the once-busy scene.

Some miners stayed on, but thirty years later they, too, were dealt another blow which no one could have foreseen.

The Levant Mine, on the North coast of Cornwall, was the scene of a terrible catastrophe.

A few men were lucky. Some–including a boy–were rescued, but thirty-one miners were crushed and killed.

With this disaster, the heart seemed to have gone out of Cornish mining, and for years it seemed over and done with, although the tin was always there below the ground.

There is still tin in Cornwall–millions of pounds' worth, some experts say. But Cornwall has changed completely. It is tourist country now, and holidaymakers would hate to see it become an industrial centre again.

Today, heather covers the scars left by three hundred mines, and the roaring engine-houses are now just picturesque reminders of the days when Cornwall stood for Tin.

Tonga

As our tiny plane came hedge-hopping over the coconuts and landed on the grass, we knew right away that our Expedition to Tonga was going to be full of surprises! Above the noise of the engine we could hear guitars and singing, and through the little windows we could see hundreds of people who appeared to be having some sort of party!

At the Royal Palace we met Princess Pilolevu. Later, Lesley learned to bash out strips of tree bark to make the special Tongan cloth. Stuck together with tapioca paste and then painted, it makes an enormous picture. This one's hanging now by the BBC canteen.

It's like that every time a plane lands at Tongatapu Airport. Dozens of Tongan families come along to wave to their friends and to see if anyone new has turned up.

We didn't know anyone on the whole island, but the moment we stepped out of the plane, it seemed that everybody knew us! Garlands of beautiful tropical flowers were put round our necks and we were greeted just like old friends. Our English names must have been spotted from the passenger list and visitors from Britain always get a special welcome—perhaps because they've come so far, for Tonga's 12,000 miles away on the other side of the world. As well as flowers, nearly everyone was wearing skirts, both the men and the women. It's Tongan national dress and it's topped off with a mat worn round the waist called a Ta'ovala. Some of the mats were made of shells, but most of them were plaited leaves. Pretty tatty some of them were, too—black with age and full of holes—but these are the best ones, handed down from father to son and prized as family heirlooms.

Tonga has a nickname—the Friendly Islands. That's what Captain Cook, the great explorer, called them when he became the first Englishman to land there 200 years ago. Just like us, he was greeted with flowers and music, and ever since that day, Tongans and Britons have stayed friends. Like our country, Tonga is a kingdom, so of course, there's a palace in Nuku'alofa, the Capital city. King Taufa'ahau Tupou IV lives there with his family and our Queen Elizabeth has been there to stay with him. It's a wooden building, painted white with a red roof, and although it may be the smallest palace in the world, we thought it quite the nicest. The King had just left for a trip to Britain when we arrived, but it was a very exciting moment when we had an invitation to visit the Palace—not just as tourists, but as guests of the King's daughter, the Princess Pilolevu. She's about the same age as Princess Anne, and a sportswoman, too. It's not horses for her, though, it's basketball! She captains one of the best teams in Tonga as well as having a regular job teaching in a school just next door to the Palace.

The Princess told us all sorts of things to look out for on our expedition, like the amazing blow holes along the coast where the giant Pacific rollers smash into the coral reef and spurt jets of water 60 feet into the air. She told us, too, about the Royal Flying Foxes. They're fruit bats—hundreds of thousands of them—that hang from the trees in a village called Kolovai. No one quite knows why they all settled there, but by a centuries-old tradition, they're the King's property. No one's allowed to hunt them except him, and as he doesn't want to, they live there very happily under his protection.

When we were exploring one day, we came across the village of Haveluliku. It was very attractive with white fences and beautiful flowers.

When we arrived, all the men were at work. If you've got time to spare in Tonga, and you come across some people who are busy, it's the custom to go and give them a hand. Pete thought he'd join the builders and he was pretty surprised to find that the building materials were leaves grabbed from the nearest trees, plaited into walls and sewn together

It's a great honour to be invited by the chiefs to a Kava ceremony. The only snag is drinking the stuff! It's a peppery drink that tastes like it looks — washing-up water! One sip and your tongue goes numb!

Recipe for a Tongan feast: Dig a hole in the ground, then fill it with hot stones. Wrap exotic fruit and vegetables in leaves and place on stones. Thatch the the hole with banana stalks and leaves, and plait some plates from palm fronds. Dig up and eat!

with palm fronds threaded through a giant-sized wooden needle!

Meanwhile John thought he'd help pick coconuts. Every family in the village gets through about 35 nuts a day. They eat them, drink the milk, and make handy cups and bowls out of the shells, so gathering the nuts is a non-stop job. Nobody climbs the trees to harvest them though. Tongans wait till they fall and then chuck them into a horse-drawn cart that's shared by everyone in the village. When the village decides to buy some sort of treat, like a transistor radio or a lawn mower, everybody contributes some coconuts to sell to the Government for export. But mostly Tongans don't worry too much about money because nearly everything they need they can grow in their villages. There's pigs and hens, and marvellous fruit and vegetables, and even their special cloth, Tapa, grows on trees!

All the ladies in the village make tapa, and Lesley discovered what a very tricky job it is. It starts out as a strip of bark which has to be bashed flat with special wooden hammers. Then when it's dried, the strips are stuck together with tapioca and decorated with beautiful patterns of birds and trees and animals. The ladies join together to make the huge ceremonial tapa cloths that are their traditional gifts to their Chiefs. We were delighted when we were presented with the cloth that Lesley helped to make. It's enormous, and at this very moment, it's hanging over the entrance to the BBC canteen so that everyone who works at the Television Centre can enjoy looking at it.

Our best day of all was when the villagers of Haveluliku invited us to a feast. It began with a special ceremony—drinking a curious brew called

Kava. Only the chiefs attend the Kava ceremony so we three were very honoured when we were invited to sit down with them. Kava is the powdered root of a tree and the drink's made rather like tea or coffee by pouring water on to a plant. The girls of the village make the drink for the men, and it has to be done in just the right way. Salote and Alice first of all ground the Kava with stones. Then they put it in a big wooden bowl called a tanoa. Next, a bucket full of water was poured in and the bits of wood and bark were swirled around and strained with a bunch of raffia. Salote did this very slowly and carefully while the chiefs kept a very beady eye on the proceedings.

The result looked nauseating—a bowl full of gritty water the colour of mud—and we were going to have to drink it! It's considered very insulting not to drink Kava when it's offered, so when our names were called, we bravely drained our coconut shells to the last drop. But like a lot of things you dread but can't avoid, it turned out not so bad as we'd feared. It tasted exactly as it looked—peppery water—so strong that it made our tongues go numb, and funnily enough, in a tropical climate that's quite refreshing!

While we were drinking with the chiefs, everyone else in Haveluliku was busy preparing the feast. Early that morning the men had dug a pit in the ground, lit a fire in it and piled it with stones. When they were just about red hot, they wrapped the meat and vegetables up in leaves and put them straight on the stones. There are no oven dishes or saucepans needed—just a few banana fronds laid on top of the food, a wet piece of sacking and on top of that a few good spadesful of earth to keep the heat in.

While the food's cooking, the ladies get busy

Feasting in Tonga is the world's finest way
to picnic! There's music to entertain you
whilst the food cooks and everyone dances
barefoot on the grass. When the feast
arrives it's a mouth-watering spread of
yams, pigs, water melon and sticky syrup
dumplings. And you eat the lot with your
fingers!

plaiting the plates from leaves and carving little
dishes from bamboo stalks. The plaited plates are
called polas and as soon as the men have dug up the
dinner, the ladies set to work arranging the food on
them. They take as much trouble to make them look
nice as we would laying the table for a special party.

The results were spectacular–bright green leaf
polas piled high with roast pig, chicken, banana leaf
parcels full of steaming hot dumplings in honey, and
slices of pink water melon to wash it all down.

Before we ate, a long grace was said. Tongans
are very religious people and wouldn't dream of
eating before they've thanked God for the food. Then
we all tucked in, picking out tit-bits with our fingers.
There was a mountain of food and we could have
eaten as much as we liked. Only the chiefs and their
guests are allowed to sit round the polas, and as
everyone else has to wait till they've finished, it's
good manners in Tonga to leave plenty over for the
rest of the village.

Some of the lads entertained us with singing while
we ate–and after the feast, Lesley had a great
surprise. The girls had made her garlands and a grass
skirt and they asked her to dance.

Soon, half the village was dancing and us with
them. It was great fun and we were thoroughly
enjoying ourselves–when it happened! One minute
there was a clear blue sky, the next a deafening clap
of thunder and the tropical rain came down in
buckets! In seconds we were soaked, but nobody
minded. The Tongans just fell about laughing! And
that perhaps is what we shall always remember about
our summer expedition to the South Pacific–a
kingdom full of smiling people who made us welcome
and certainly lived up to their centuries-old
nickname–the Friendly Islanders.

Do you remember these Father Christmas decorations? Pete and I made the big one to deliver the family presents in his sack, the middle one to bring the cards, and the little one to hold the crackers in the middle of the party table. They're all made the same way. Here's how to do it:

GETTING READY FOR CHRISTMAS

1 For a middle-sized Father Christmas, like we're making, start by pasting four double sheets of newspaper in layers and finish off with a sheet of brown paper. If you're going to make a giant Father Christmas, make another piece this size and sticky-tape the two together. Leave the paper until it dries hard.

2 The body is a cone shape, so you'll need to mark a curve. We made a giant-sized set of compasses like Val did when she made a Christmas tree. Tie a string to a pencil and drawing-pin the other end to the corner of the paper. Move the pencil gently in case the drawing-pin comes out. Cut out along the mark.

3 Fold the paper into a cone shape and fasten it firmly with sticky tape or glue. This job's easier with two people—one to hold and one to stick! Snip the top off the cone, because this is where the head and neck will slot in.

4 Now cover the body with red crêpe paper. Tuck the paper neatly down the neck and round the bottom edge and glue on the inside for a neat finish. Don't worry about the join because this will get hidden in a minute.

5 It's cotton-wool trimming that hides the join. Stick some round the neck and the bottom of the red cloak, too.

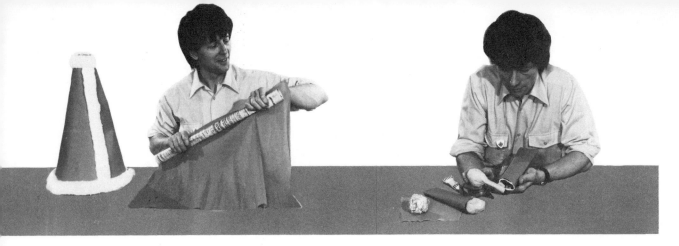

6 The arms are made from a tube of newspaper. Roll a whole double sheet up with a layer of red crêpe paper on the outside. One tube will be enough for both arms.

7 Twist some newspaper into a ball to make the hands. Cover them with pink crêpe paper and slip them into the arms with a dab of glue to keep them firmly in place. Glue the arms into place by the fur collar.

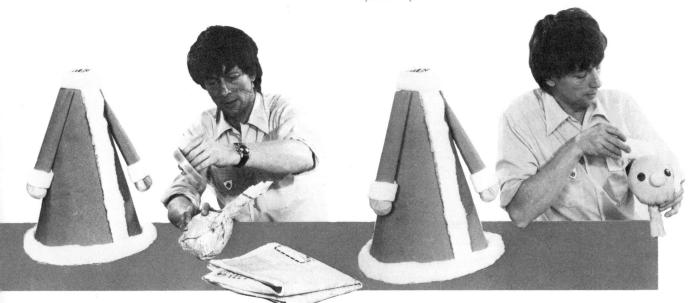

8 Next get a big ball of newspaper ready to make the head. Wind sticky tape round the neck to stop it coming apart.

9 Cover the head with a sheet of crêpe paper. For the nose, we stuck on a ping-pong ball painted pink. The eyes are black sticky-backed plastic, but buttons or black paint would be just as good. Stick on some cotton-wool hair.

10 Father Christmas's beard is a triangle of cotton wool stuck straight under his nose! That's why we didn't bother giving him a mouth! His hat is made from a cone of red crêpe paper trimmed with cotton-wool fur.

We gave our Father Christmases belts and buckles for a finishing touch—a paper one for Big, and real ones for Middle and Little. We made sacks, too, out of an old piece of material, but strong brown paper bags work just as well. We didn't give Little a sack. He's got a bunch of crackers instead, tied to his arm with a string of tinsel. Our Father Christmases looked great in the "Blue Peter" studio. They'd look just as good in your house, too, and if you pack them away carefully when the holidays are over, you can bring them out year after year.

THE CASE OF
THE MISSING LINK

Can you solve this case. Five careless mistakes gave away the crooks. We spotted them. Can you?

"Security – that's the most important thing, Bob," said Detective Inspector McCann as their black Presidential Rolls-Royce purred down the M4 from London Airport to the Television Centre.

As he spoke, his eyes never left the small blue mini van twenty yards ahead that was carrying the President of Kosenkrantz and his Aide, Colonel Duffinger. The President was on his way to take part in an important political interview with Heron Night in the BBC's "Diorama" programme. The secret plan was that this inconspicuous vehicle would slip unseen into the back entrance of the studios, whilst the President's Rolls-Royce swept up to the main gates. Bob, who luckily was exactly the same build as the President, was to act as decoy. With his uncle to guard him, he felt quite confident, even though that very morning at the

airport an attempt at assassination had already been made.

Detective Inspector McCann, however, was not so certain as he fingered a small gold link from a wristwatch chain.

"I'd have had that blighter, Bob," he muttered, "if that fool Duffinger hadn't got in my way."

"He was only trying to help, Uncle," replied Bob. "When he saw that man grab for the President, he must have been as worried as we were."

"All the same," rasped McCann, "that attacker is still at large, and we can't be certain he won't strike again. Keep your eyes skinned when we get to the studios. This gold link's the only clue we've got."

The plan worked. The President and his Aide were now safely installed in the BBC's

VIP suite, and Bob and McCann made their way up to the Diorama studio. This was McCann's chance to check his security arrangments. Heron Night, the famous interviewer, came bustling up.

"Everything all right, Inspector?"

McCann nodded and then looked up into the studio lights.

"Who's allowed on that platform up there, Mr Night?" he queried.

"Never been up there myself," laughed Night. "It's just for the electrician chappies who set the lights."

"I'll just nip up and have a look round, sir," said McCann. "We can't take any chances!"

As he climbed the narrow iron stairs, he couldn't help thinking that the gantry, with its bird's eye view of the studio floor, would be a good place to hide a marksman.

Chief Electrician Tony Kingsfold was waiting at the top of the ladder.

"Sorry, sir," he said. "You'll have to go. Only electricians allowed up here."

McCann produced his identity card.

"McCann, Special Branch," he explained.

"Checking up are you, Governor?"

"That's right. Do you always work on Diorama?"

"No, normally on Wednesdays I'm working on Blue Peter, but today being special, they asked me to come over after my lunch break and help out because the President was coming."

"Have you been here all afternoon?" queried McCann.

"Of course I have, Guv. As you know, no one's been allowed to leave the studio since the President's mini van arrived at the back entrance. I've been stuck up 'ere for hours."

"What's the time now?" asked McCann.

Kingsfold took a watch out of his top pocket. "Quarter to eight, Guv."

"I see you've broken your wristwatch," said McCann. "How did that happen?"

"I broke it when I was luggin' one of them 5-volt lamps up here first fing this mornin'. Dead weight, they are."

McCann looked over the gantry rail at the technicians on the floor. "Diorama will be on the air soon. What are the cameramen doing now?"

"Loading the film in their cameras, I expect, sir. They've got to be ready when the red transmission lights start flashing."

At that moment the studio door opened and the Floor Assistant ushered in the President of Kosenkrantz and Colonel Duffinger.

"Please sit here, Mr President," he said, and introduced him to Heron Night. "If you would come with me, Colonel, I'll find you a chair just out of camera."

"Absolute silence everywhere," called the Floor Manager.

The President sipped a glass of water as Heron rehearsed his introduction.

"Stand by everybody," shouted the Floor Manager and raised his hand ready to cue the speakers.

"I'm afraid I'll have to ask you to leave now, Guv," said Kingsfold. "No one's allowed up 'ere during transmission except me."

"All the same, I think I'll stick around," replied McCann.

On the studio floor Bob glanced up and saw the two men deep in conversation. Night smiled at the camera.

"Good evening and welcome to Diorama. Tonight I have with me in the studio . . ."

"Look 'ere Guv," said the electrician, "you'll have to go."

"Sh!" hissed McCann.

Suddenly the electrician's hand flashed out and McCann was looking at a fat silencer on the end of a .38″ pistol.

"All right, copper! 'Ave it your own way. You first, and then the President!"

"You won't get away with this," snapped McCann.

"Oh yes I will! Duffinger's in this, too. Caught in the crossfire with his gun and mine, no one in this studio stands a chance."

In a flash McCann kicked at the electrician's wrist. He gave a scream of pain and the pistol flew over the gantry rail and fell with a clatter at the feet of Duffinger. Heron Night didn't bat an eyelid. Suavely he carried on the interview. Then Colonel Duffinger grabbed for the pistol but Bob hurled himself on him in a flying tackle.

". . . thank you, Mr President, and from me, Heron Night, until next week goodnight!"

The signature tune blared out as Bob and Duffinger grappled on the floor. The red light on the camera snapped out, and the calm smile left Night's face.

"What the devil's going on, here,?" he snapped.

"I'll tell you what's going on," said McCann, appearing with a hand-cuffed electrician. "There's just been an attempt on the President's life."

"But . . ." faltered Heron.

"Don't worry, sir. It's all over now."

"How did you find out, Uncle?" cried Bob. "What put you on to them?"

"This so-called electrician made five very foolish mistakes – and that solved the mystery of the missing link!"

Did you spot the five mistakes? Check your answers on page 76.

There can't be many people who are owners of a gold motorbike, but when World Speedway champion Ivan Mauger visited the Blue Peter Studio, he brought one gleaming all over with real gold plate, even down to the sparking plugs!

Friends in America promised Ivan they'd gold-plate his bike if he won the World Championship three times in succession—they'd already chrome-plated it after his first win and silver-plated it after he'd gained the title for the second time. Ivan's actually been World Champion four times and he won the title three times in succession between 1968 and 1970.

You have to have real guts to be a speedway champion—it's a sport that's dirty, dangerous and fast. John and I will never forget the hairy day we spent training with the Hackney Hawks and their team Manager and Chief Instructor—Len Silver.

2 Our first lesson was how to do a racing start. You don't get a push start for a race—you line up with the engine running and the experts get away with tremendous acceleration. But a racing start has to be safe as well as fast—the big danger is that the back wheel has a tendency to climb underneath the front wheel and tip you over backwards.

1 Len Silver gave us a few tips about the controls of a speedway bike. There are no brakes and no gears, the only controls are the clutch and the throttle.

3 The technique is to release the clutch suddenly and use a lot of throttle—this starts the back wheel spinning. Whatever happens, it *mustn't* grip. At the same time you get all your weight pressing on the handlebars, and as the bike moves, you slide back with it.

6 Our invitation race took place that night—in front of thousands of Hackney Speedway fans!
My bike wouldn't start at all, so I was given a substitute which felt very strange. It seemed more powerful than my practice bike and I wasn't sure if I could control it—but with thousands of spectators, I just had to carry on and try my best.

4 Cornering came next. For this you don't sit in your saddle, you stand on the foot rests, putting your left foot out, keeping your right leg straight, you put a little bit of weight on your left foot— which is why speedway riders have steel shoes fitted to the bottom of their boots so that they can slide easily over the ground. As you turn your throttle on, the back wheel slides outwards and you and the bike go round the corner in a nice slide.
Deliberately skidding like this is the quickest and safest way of getting round bends. But it's something you can't possibly do on a push bike.

7 Disaster struck after the first lap. In an all-out attempt to catch Terry and Mark, who'd streaked ahead of John and me, my bike started to slide and in a flash, I was out of control.

5 Len said we'd done so well, he was going to put us in a race, and our two opponents, 14-year-old Terry Barclay and Mark Coombs, came up to say hello. They'd been training for the past six months, so Johnny and I didn't rate our chances very highly.

8 Thanks to my crash helmet and my protective leathers, there was no harm done—and the bike was undamaged, too. Feeling your back wheel starting to slide from under you is quite frightening —your natural reaction is to slow down, but that would be fatal. You must keep your speed *up*, and that's the hardest thing to learn.
Speedway may look easy, but John and I feel quite happy leaving it to Ivan Mauger and the experts!

LESLEY SAYS

"THERE'S MORE TO JOHN NOAKES THAN MEETS THE EYE..."

When I first met John a year ago, I thought he was kind, with a terrific sense of humour, and a rugged North-country determination that made him climb chimneys and jump out of aeroplanes. But when I got to know him a bit better, I realised that beneath the toughness and the clowning and the down-to-earth practical man, there was a real creative artist. Take his hobby of making glass trees for instance . . .

I've always been fascinated by trees— winter trees I mean with black, intertwining branches standing stark against the sky. I used to draw them when I was young; not realistic trees, but impressions of twisting, interlacing branches. Strangely enough it was

My trees have to be pulled and twisted into shape at a temperature of 1700°C.

When I've made the branches, I weld them into the main trunk. Too much heat and they melt away!

I enjoy deciding where to weld the branches so that the finished design looks balanced.

the wife of one of the Blue Peter film directors that got me on to making glass trees. Pauline Cowdy came out with us for the day when her husband, Harry, and I were filming Spalding Flower Parade. While Harry and the cameraman were working out the next shot, Pauline and I got chatting and she told me that she was a glass artist.

That night I telephoned a friend of hers called Eric White, and the next Tuesday I joined the evening class he runs, only a few miles from the Blue Peter studios.

Under Eric's instruction I started experimenting with glass trees. As far as we know, no one has ever tried it before. To start with, we had to find the right kind of glass, one with a very high melting temperature so that it will stretch and bend and twist when heated, but will cool down rapidly without breaking while it stays in the shape that you've made. I found that quartz glass which comes from a mountain in Brazil will only soften at about 1700 degrees centigrade. It takes two powerful oxy-gas burners to produce that kind of heat.

I hold the glass rod at either end with the middle in the white-hot flame and as it begins to melt, I pull and twist it into the shape I like.

The exciting thing is that you've got to make instant decisions as soon as you feel the glass beginning to bend. There's no turning back once you begin, and if you hold it in the flame a second too long, it will all melt away.

When I've made all the branches, I weld them into the main trunk. The nearer you get to completion, the easier it is to knock off a finished branch while you're trying to add a new one. I've found by bitter experience that it's no good rushing the final stages.

Once all the branches are in position, I sand blast the whole tree in a special cabinet. This makes it opaque and frosty so that you can see the outline of the branches.

We're discovering new techniques all the time. Recently I put some powdered glass into a salt-cellar and shook it through the flame on to the tree. After sand blasting it looked just like bark!

It gives me a lot of pleasure working with glass. I used to be an aircraft fitter years ago and I've always enjoyed doing things with my hands. But best of all I like trying to do something that no one has ever done before. You may not like my trees, but you can't compare them with any others!

Eric White has taught me everything I know about glass.

When the tree is complete, I put it in a sand blaster.

It comes out frosty and opaque so you can see the branches.

BRASS ONLY

WATCH STRAP

TREASURE HUNT
BLUE PETER

255 tons! That's a rough estimate of the avalanche of treasure that was sent to us from all corners of the country as the result of our appeal for our Blue Peter Old People's Centre. Thanks to you, we've been able to give badly needed help to elderly and disabled people all over Britain. Here's how it all began.

There are 9 million people in Britain over the age of 60—that's one sixth of the whole population. Hundreds and thousands of them stay cooped up in their rooms with nowhere to go, and Old People's Clubs and Centres are desperately badly needed. Places that are open every day of the week, where old people can drop in for a cup of tea or a game of dominoes, a chat with their friends and a good hot meal.

In a High Street in Deptford, for instance, we discovered there'd been nowhere for old folk to go for the past two years. There *was* a club there once, but since it had been closed down, it hadn't been replaced. And then we heard about Edwards Bakery—an empty delapidated shop that would make an ideal Club House if only it could be renovated and redecorated. Volunteers had been trying to sell old clothes and trinkets to raise the money to do this, but it would have taken years and years to have got anything like enough.

When we went to investigate, things looked grim. The whole building was derelict—full of rubble and junk and relics of the old days—great gaping holes where the huge ovens had once stood, and things like a long-handled baker's shovel for moving the bread. But although there was an enormous replastering and painting job to be done, underneath the mess, the brick walls and ceilings were perfectly sound.

The garden looked just as awful as the house, it was knee high in weeds and rubbish, and there was the mammoth job of renovating *that*, too.

But we knew if only we could raise the funds, there could be a complete transformation. We'd not only have a superb Club House, our Blue Peter Old People's Centre would have its own walled garden, too.

1 The outside of the old bakery before it was transformed into our first Blue Peter Old People's Centre.

2 We discovered that beneath the rubble, the brick walls and ceilings were perfectly sound.

3 The garden before we started work—knee high in weeds and rubbish.

4 Four weeks later it was spick and span with the flower beds full of plants donated by viewers.

It was then we had our Treasure Hunt idea—not the ordinary kind where you dig for gold and silver—we asked for things like old propelling pencils and key rings, broken watch straps, odd earrings, bashed-up old picture frames and fire irons, worn-out thimbles and purses, and old metal buttons—the sort of junk that's pushed to the back of drawers and cupboards and forgotten about.

Within days, our collecting depot was piled high with mail bags and parcels. The sorting was very complicated—there was such a variety of treasure it all had to be sorted and stored in sections—like brass, watchstraps and thimbles, etc. But it was worth all the trouble, because the response was better than our wildest dreams. By January 1st, we'd made it! We'd achieved not only our target, but a fleet of four Hot Dinner Vans as well. By February 12th, the number of vans had risen to eight!

The idea of the vans is to help people who can't manage to get out to a Day Centre, or to cook for themselves. Between them, the vans, based at Deptford, Birmingham, Greenock, Cardiff, Liverpool, Middlesbrough, Belfast and Bristol, deliver 800 hot meals a day. At a time when there are so many tragic stories about Old Age pensioners literally starving to death because they can't manage to cook for themselves, there's no doubt that the need for these vans is enormous.

Most of the treasure was scrap metal that was melted down into valuable alloy ingots. But the parcel sorting had been so thorough, we'd set aside some treasure of a different kind, things like antiques and jewellery, rare coins, glass, china and silver. After experts gave them another going over, we held three public auctions that raised even more money. The most valuable of the coins and medals were sold at Sotheby's, and on Tuesday, April 17th, we held a complete Treasure Hunt Sale at Phillips that raised £6,159. That, put together with the rest of the Sale money, meant that on April 19th, we were able to announce we'd be able to get our second Blue Peter Old People's Centre!

But that's not all. With extra donations still coming in, we are going to be able to give a hundred Old People seaside holidays at the Isle of Wight, and we may even be able to add to our Hot Dinner Van fleet, too.

Altogether, life will be a lot happier for a great many old people, which is why we think this must certainly have been one of the best-ever Treasure Hunts!

5 Based at Deptford, Birmingham, Greenock, Cardiff, Liverpool, Middlesbrough, Belfast and Bristol, our Hot Dinner Vans will deliver 800 meals a day to housebound old people.

THATCHER'S MATE

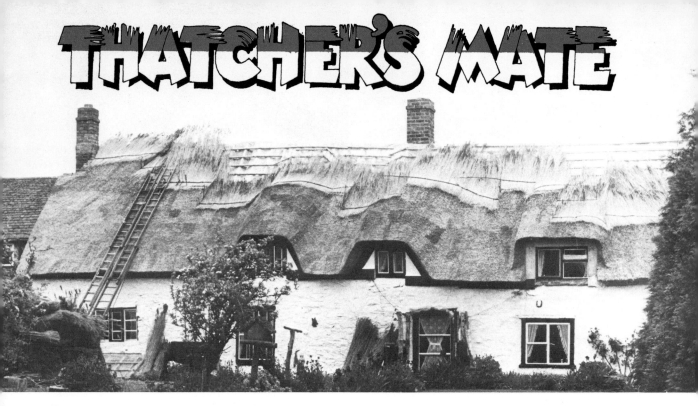

Compared with climbing 267-foot tower cranes or painting 308-foot power-station chimneys, an assignment a mere 20 feet high sounds a bit of a flea bite. But helping to thatch this roof was one of the hardest day's work I've ever done!

Thatching is the oldest of all building crafts—it goes back hundreds of years, even before the Norman conquest, and the techniques and the tools the thatcher uses have hardly changed to this very day.

But nowadays thatch is expensive compared with slate or stone, and thatchers are few and far between. I'd never seen one at work before I visited the Leicestershire village of Swithland, a few months ago, where a 15th-century cottage was being completely stripped and rethatched for the first time since it was built. Mr Wally Payne, who owns Pit Close Cottage, invited me down for the day, and quite honestly, if I'd realised what I was in for, I might have had second thoughts! But like most people, I was pretty ignorant about thatching. I'd no idea how much really hard work was involved.

When I arrived, the garden was strewn with piles of black twisted rafters. They'd been holding up the thatch for 500 years, but most of the old wood had to be taken down, and carpenter Terry Holt had put a new framework up in its place.

Another thing that made Pit Close Cottage unusual was that it's a cruck cottage. Originally the trunks of five stout oak trees had been split down the middle and used as arches to hold up the walls and form the shape of the roof. The distance between the crucks was always 16 feet—but today Pit Close Cottage has only the three centre crucks still standing.

1 Bundles of Norfolk reed were stacked on the lawn at the back of Pit Close Cottage.

2 My first job as Thatcher's Mate was to carry the reed up the ladders on the roof.

3 Marcus Davis showed me how to secure them with thatching pins.

4 The reeds can be sewn with tough cord, as well as nailed.

5 This leggett was used to knock the reeds into position.

6 Hazel rods split with a Brotch hook were used to decorate the porch.

I was amazed to hear from Wally, that these three crucks which had supported the very first roof at the turn of the 15th century were so strong they didn't need replacing. It made me wonder how many of our modern buildings would be in such fine condition in the year 2473 AD.

The day I visited Swithland the new roof was at its halfway stage and Marcus Davis, the thatcher, had been hard at work for two months. At one point he'd had to stop completely because the supplies of Norfolk reed had been held up— so Marcus was keen to keep thatching whilst he showed me what he was doing—and he got me joining in, too. Wearing two stout, leather knee-caps and my sleeves rolled up, I was ready for action and all set to be a Thatcher's Mate.

My first job was carrying bundles of Norfolk reed up the ladders on the roof to where Marcus was working. If you've ever had a holiday on the Broads, you'll have seen the reed growing in the marshes. Nowadays it's cultivated especially for thatching, and it's far superior to straw or wheat reed—lasting two or three times as long. The bundles were stacked high on Wally's back lawn. Marcus told me to balance three or four of them on my shoulder and use my other hand for climbing the ladder. By the time I reached the top, I felt I could do with a shoulder pad as well as knee pads!

Marcus secured the bundles with thatching pins to stop them sliding off the roof — then after I cut the cord, or bond around the first bundle, he slid it under a thin hazel rod called a sway. Rows of these sways were running horizontally all along the roof, but each row was hidden by the next layer or course of reeds.

Thatchers, I discovered, always start at the bottom and work up. The reed is palmed up by hand to get the ends level, which can be quite painful, and then knocked into position with a leggett—a square block with rows of nails sticking out like bristles in a brush. There were literally dozens of these special words to learn—by the end of the day I'd acquired a whole new vocabulary! Marcus showed me how he hooked thatching nails on to the sway and drove them into the rafters underneath. The reeds can be sewn with tough cord as well as nailed, but whichever the method used, the reed is fixed so securely to the rafters, it'll never blow off—not even in a gale. The thatch was an overall thickness of 12 inches, and although Marcus knew instinctively the depth was even, he checked every so often by measuring it with a thatching pin.

The top of the roof was going to be decorated with a cap of sedge grass after the reeds had been cut level with an eaves knife. I could see how this would look because the front porch had already been finished off in this way and decorated with liggers—more pieces of split hazel rods. Marcus' partner, Leo, had split most of the hazels by hand, using a blood-curdling-looking knife called a Brotch hook.

No wonder thatching is a long, slow job. There are no short cuts and no machinery to make the work easy. It's tough, dirty, back-breaking work, and although I'd only helped for a few hours, I felt I'd really earned the mugs of tea Wally made for us!

But there are rewards, too. It's a marvellous feeling to create something with your own hands, and a newly-thatched roof looks really beautiful. And apart from looks, thatch has a big advantage over other roofs — it keeps a cottage warm in winter and cool in summer, and no rain or snow can penetrate the tightly packed reeds.

P.S. Two months later Wally invited me back to Pit Close Cottage. The finished result was superb and I felt quite proud to have played a small part in producing it when I was Thatcher's Mate for a day. The next time you're in the country, watch out for a thatcher at work. After reading this, you'll be able to surprise your friends with your knowledge of Brotch hooks, Liggers, Leggetts, Courses and Sways!

ROMAN REPORTER

When I was in Rome last summer, at the very heart of one of the greatest Empires the world has ever known, I became fascinated by the ancient Romans.

For one thing, even though they were living 2,000 years ago, I could see with my own eyes all kinds of relics—buildings, beautiful mosaics—even kitchen pots and jewellery, reminders of how the Romans lived and worked. Bit by bit, archaeologists and historians have pieced together all the evidence, and now their picture of Roman times is pretty accurate.

But you don't have to travel to Italy to do this kind of detective work, and I was delighted when I was asked to report for Blue Peter from two places in Britain where there had been great Roman settlements—the City of York and Hadrian's Wall.

ALONG THE WALL

The Emperor Hadrian planned to build a wall to mark the end of the Roman Empire.

Ten thousand men worked for two years building the wall to keep at bay the hostile tribes of the North.

The Romans called England Britannia—it was the northernmost province of their Empire, and they built a wall across Northumberland, stretching from coast to coast to keep at bay the hostile tribes of the North whom the Romans never conquered, although they kept on trying. This amazing feat of engineering was the bold idea of one man—Hadrian, Emperor of Rome.

Before the wall was built, he made a grand tour of his vast Empire. When he came to Britain he was told about the Caledonians and the warring tribes in the North, and when he looked at the map, he said:

"The Roman Empire shall end *here*—at the narrowest part of Britain. We will build a wall to mark the end of the Empire."

So they set to work. In all ten thousand men worked for two solid years building the wall for Hadrian. And today, eighteen hundred and fifty years later, parts of it still stand. In its day, it was three times as high as it is now, for over the centuries much of it has collapsed, but even so, it's an unforgettable sight.

It loops the Northumberland countryside sprawling like a snake over the hills. It climbs rocky crags, and skirts moorland lakes.

Today the wall is quiet and deserted. I walked along it for miles, not meeting a soul, and at first it was difficult to believe that this was once the scene of bustling organised activity, as the

Forts were built to garrison the troops like this one at Housesteads. These posts held the wooden granary floor clear of the ground.

Roman soldiers went about their duties.

Originally, the wall was fifteen feet high, and eight feet wide, and sentries patrolled the top, protected by battlements. At night they used torches for signalling, so if there was any suspicious movement from the hostile Caledonians, the whole wall was alerted within minutes.

A Roman mile was a thousand paces, a little shorter than an English mile–so the Wall was eighty *Roman* miles long. Every mile they built a stronghold, called a mile-castle, which held fifty men.

There were seventeen forts along the Wall, which were like garrison towns, and these were where the men lived. It was a tough tour of duty–the men signed on for twenty-five years, and if they survived they retired with honours and a grant of land.

They lived in barrack-room blocks, holding sixty to a hundred men, and every day, each section queued outside the granary to receive its ration of corn. The soldiers baked their own bread from this, and ate it with meat or dried fruit.

At the fort the Romans called Vercovium, which is known as Housesteads today, I walked along 1850-year-old streets, and traced the outline of the buildings. In Rome the ruins I had seen were often of marble, with beautiful mosaic pavements. There was nothing like that here–everything was very severe and bare with nothing in the way of luxury or comfort.

To while away the time, the troops spent hours drinking and gambling, and playing dice. I actually held a set of dice, and dice cups, the Romans had played with that had been dug up near the wall. And I went into the ruins of a Temple which the soldiers had built, where they met together to offer sacrifices to Mithras, the Sun God. Many of them had come from sunny Mediterranean countries, like Spain or Morocco. On bitter cold December days, like the day when

There were 17 forts along the wall, and the soldiers lived in barrack-room blocks holding 60 to 100 men.

To while away the time, the troops spent hours drinking, gambling and playing dice.

This set of dice and the cup were dug up near the wall. They're on display at the Corbridge Museum.

I was there, they must have longed to be back in their own warm lands.

I was tremendously impressed by the Wall. I had seen nothing like it, not even in Rome itself, and as I explored, I could easily imagine that those Romans were still there, marching with their glittering eagles along the loneliest frontier of their great Empire.

DOWN THE SEWERS

The extraordinary thing is, people are still making discoveries about the Romans, although they left Britain more than 1500 years ago.

For instance, in York last year, a new office block was being built, and as the excavators cleared the ground, they unearthed signs of a major Roman settlement. York was an important town, even back in Roman times, but this was something quite new. The builders had to get on with their work, but they gave the archaeologists two weeks to investigate.

Like a shot, I went up there to report for the programme, and I was amazed to find that the discoveries were not just pieces of tiles and pottery. Between them the archaeologists and the builders unearthed a whole Roman sewage system, dating back to the year AD 200!

Peter Addyman, the Director of the York Archaeological Trust, took me on a specially conducted tour. We had to wear gum boots and oil skins and crash helmets. After crawling through a manhole and climbing 17 feet below pavement level, we splashed through water and crouched double as we made our way along a maze of underground passages.

Our tunnel went on for fifty yards, then it opened out. Peter told me these passages were the actual sewers, serving the bath block for the officers' quarters, and the camp latrines.

"Did the Romans have flush lavatories?" I asked.

"Well, sometimes they had streams running under the lavatory seat, but here they had holes over the sewer system," he replied.

I looked suspiciously at the floors, covered with something that looked like mud.

"As we are in a sewer, Peter," I asked, "*is

that mud on the floor?"

"No–you're quite right! It's not mud, it's excreta. We've had it analysed. And also there are the bodies of hundreds of sewer beetles who seemed to like living in those sorts of condition."

"Extraordinary," I murmured.

Stiff and aching from our hunched-up positions, we slowly crawled back along the passages that had once been Roman drains.

My investigations here seemed a far cry from exploring marble palaces under the blue skies of Rome!

ROMAN BANQUET

The banquet was the high spot of the Roman's day, and after all my investigations into Roman Britain, and my visit to Rome, I decided to try to give one.

For one day, we transformed the Blue Peter studio into a Roman dining-room, with a tiled floor and marble pillars, and in the middle a low table with couches on three sides. The Romans called a dining-room a "triclinium", which means three couches.

Lesley and Peter, who were my guests, arrived looking very smart in cool, loose robes that the Romans would wear for parties, and we all took our places.

The Romans ate lying down, propped up on one elbow. They used their fingers a great deal, because it is impossible to use knives and forks when you're lying down, and they used napkins to wipe their fingers.

They used the napkins for something else, too. If you liked something very much, it was perfectly good manners to wrap some of it up in your napkin to take home.

We started with a Roman dish that's still a top favourite–hors d'oeuvres–eggs, sardines, mushrooms, olives, and all sorts of delicious things.

Of course, the Roman hostess didn't cook the food or wait on the guests herself–she had slaves to do that.

John had very kindly offered to be the slave at my banquet. He took away the used dishes

and brought in great mounds of roast meat, and chicken, and pigeons, serving them all at the empty fourth side of the table.

Then he went round pouring wine into goblets very like ones still in use today. He added water to the wine – the Romans always did this, and many Italians do to this day.

Roman puddings were marvellous – fruit, and honey and almond cakes, and even a kind of ice-cream made from fruit juices frozen in snow kept in a special ice-house.

Sometimes the Romans were so greedy they ate enough to make themselves sick, but it didn't stop them. It just emptied their stomachs so that they could come back to the table and start eating all over again.

But we had nothing like that in our triclinium!

Everyone behaved well – we had a splendid meal and every one of us enjoyed our Roman banquet – even slave John!

Pancake party

You don't have to save pancakes for Shrove Tuesday—they're far too good to be eaten on only one day of the year. You can serve them sweet or savoury with a whole range of different fillings, and they can be cooked the day before you need them and reheated. Pancakes are made from such simple ingredients they're a useful standby if you want to give unexpected guests a snack, and they're delicious enough for party food, too.

For 12 pancakes you will need:
4 oz plain flour
2 large eggs
2 tablespoons of oil *or* melted butter
a pinch of salt
½ pint slightly warm milk

1 Beat the ingredients together, putting them in your mixing bowl in the order listed in the recipe.

2 After greasing your frying-pan with a piece of buttered paper, heat it on the stove and measure out enough mixture for one pancake.

3 Cook one side quickly, shaking the pan to prevent the batter sticking. If you daren't risk tossing, turn the pancake over with a spatula.

4 Stack your pancakes one on top of the other, covering them with a linen cloth to keep them moist.

5 Traditionally, pancakes are eaten with lemon or orange juice and sugar. Squeeze juice over the flat pancake and sprinkle a spoonful of sugar over the top. Roll the pancake up and arrange on serving dish.

6 Strawberry jam can be a very tasty filling too, and so can maple syrup or treacle.
For savoury pancakes, try fillings of chunky chicken in white sauce, or sausage and tomato sauce, cheese or flaked tuna fish.

If you want to make your pancakes the day before, wrap them in foil and reheat in the oven. Fill just before you serve them and keep warm in a fireproof dish in the oven.

UP-HELLY-AA!

The Shetlands are a long way north—as far again as from London to Edinburgh, and level with Oslo in Norway. They lie where the Atlantic and the North Sea meet, only 200 miles from the Western coast of Norway. Years ago they belonged to the Norwegian King, and perhaps it is because Shetlanders still feel the pull of their Viking past that the festival of Up-Helly-Aa began.

The winter days are short in the far North. By January it isn't light until 10.00 a.m., and by 3.00 p.m. it's beginning to get dark again. And so a great winter Festival of Fire has grown up in defiance of the dark days, and looking forward, with distant hope, to the arrival of the sun.

No one can remember when the first blazing tar barrels were trooped round the streets of Lerwick. But there are tales of people and property being accidentally burnt in the celebrations, so at the end of the last century, the tar barrels were banished and the Viking ship made its first appearance. From then onwards, the festival grew and grew, and now ships from Britain, Scandinavia and distant Russia converge on Lerwick harbour for the last Tuesday in January.

Preparations begin months before. The Viking ship that will be burnt to ashes in an hour is built with loving care. Costumes are made for the "guizers"—everyone who takes part in the

festival must be dis*guised* in some kind of mask or costume. Men from the Guizer Jarl's squad begin to grow their beards ready for the great night. They will be dressed as Vikings, with shining armour, shield and axe, and fearsome winged helmets. The Guizer Jarl controls the festival with supreme authority which no one questions. If Up-Helly-Aa ever went wrong, the whole of Lerwick could be burnt to the ground.

Only born Shetlanders can join in the festival of guizers. I was a bit disappointed when I first heard this because I rather fancied myself in a winged helmet, but the Guizer Jarl explained that if he allowed all visitors to join in, there'd be no room left for the islanders.

At midday on the last Tuesday in January, all the shops and pubs close in Lerwick. Everyone gathers in the street waiting for night to fall. The Viking ship, with its ferocious dragon's head prow, is mounted on wheels ready for its journey to the burning site. The Guizer Jarl gives a command in the dark, a Very pistol is fired and at the signal, 800 flaming torches are lit—Up-Helly-Aa has begun.

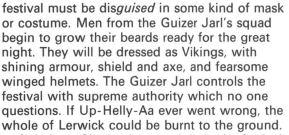

Only those born on Shetland are allowed to take part. There is a boys' squad with their own special boat.

The band strikes up and a thousand lusty voices roar out the Up-Helly-Aa song:
> "Of yore, our fiery fathers sped upon the
>   Viking Path;
> Of yore, their dreaded dragons braved the
>   ocean in its wrath;
> And we, their sons, are reaping now their
>   glory's aftermath;
> The waves are rolling on."

The Guizer Jarl gives the signal and eight hundred torches are lit—Up-Helly-Aa has begun.

Everyone in the parade is called a "guizer". The leader is called the "Guizer Jarl" and this is his "squad".

The dragon's head on the bow of the Viking Ship is beautifully made—even though it will end up being burnt to cinders.

At the burning site the torches are flung into the Viking ship.

Discipline is strict at the festival, and the Guizer Jarl's word is law.

Down the streets march the guizers—led by the Vikings of the Guizer Jarl's squad and followed by squads in every kind of costume you can imagine. There were Shetland sheep and redskins. One squad disguised as policemen, the next as garden gnomes.

Ships begin to fire rockets into the sky that is already glowing from the light of the torches. The galley is brought to its final resting place and the guizers gather round it to sing "The Norseman's Home". The Guizer Jarl gives a signal—there is a cheer and 800 torches are flung into the long, wooden ship. The funeral pyre of the Vikings begins. Soon the whole night sky glows like the Northern lights, which in the past, I'm told, have appeared to join in the celebrations.

The galley is consumed by the flames. The great dragon's head rears up in defiance, but at last it, too, keels over in the furnace and gives up the ghost.

Up-Helly-Aa, the strange, romantic festival of the Norsemen, is over for another year.

The galley is consumed by flames and Up-Helly-Aa, the strange, romantic festival of the Norsemen, is over for another year.

The Eddystone Light

1 The lighthouse that now stands high and dry on Plymouth Hoe was once washed by the most fearful seas in the world. But the story of the Eddystone Lighthouse began long before this tower was built.

2 The cruel seas that boiled over the treacherous Eddystone rock had claimed dozens of ships and hundreds of sailors' lives. But the eddying currents made it impossible for anyone to land and put up a light to warn the sailors.

I will put a light on Eddystone!

3 Until a man called Henry Winstanley, who'd lost two ships, had an idea.

4 For four long years, Winstanley struggled to get a building up on this terrifying rock.

I wouldn't mind being there in the worst storm in the world.

But what will happen in the winter storms?

5 At last it was finished. The light shone, and the sailors were safe.

6 He was there, supervising repairs, when a terrific storm blew up, the worst that anyone could remember.

7 The next morning the lighthouse had disappeared. Winstanley and his workmen were never seen alive again.

8 Two nights later, a ship was wrecked on the rocks because there was no light—the first wreck for five years. There must be another lighthouse!

9 Plans were drawn up for an oak and iron tower, firmly fixed on the rock. Its base was filled with 500 tons of stone.

11 Fire broke out! The 94-year-old lighthouse keeper and his crew were saved—but the lighthouse was burnt into the bare rock.

10 Five years later, the new elegant shape of the second lighthouse emerged, and shipping was safe again. It stood for 47 years until another terrible night . . .

That will be the model for my lighthouse

12 John Smeaton, builder and engineer, was given the task of building a new one: "An oak tree stands firm in the storm." he said. "That will be my model."

13 He built it of stone. Every block was numbered and knitted together like a giant jigsaw.

14 When it was finished, it rose 90 feet from the water. Its light could be seen for miles and it stood for 120 years.

15 This time it was not the lighthouse but the rock beneath it that eventually began to split. A fourth lighthouse was built which stands to this day by the stump of Smeaton's tower, and its light has never failed.

The LONELIEST Christmas

"Hold tight, girls! Here comes a big one," called the cox'n.

A wave that must have been twenty feet high suddenly reared up and crashed down on the cabin of the Trinity House motor boat.

The cox'n grinned sympathetically, and Ian, the "Blue Peter" cameraman, wiped the spray off his lens for the twentieth time that morning.

Lesley and I were on the last voyage to the Eddystone Lighthouse before Christmas. We were loaded with provisions for the crew of the lighthouse.

I watched the huge waves hit the stump of Smeaton's tower and fling their spray halfway up the pinnacle of today's lighthouse.

"Do you think we'll be able to land?" yelled Lesley above the roaring sea.

"I can't tell you—maybe," the cox'n shouted back.

We looked sadly at the turkey in its plastic, waterproof bag, and the Christmas cake—and the pudding—and the crackers.

"Are we going to have to take them all back?" I bellowed.

As the cox'n stared out at the lighthouse, "No," he said. "We always get them there."

If we took our little boat near the rocks, we'd surely be smashed to pieces. As I hung on, I thought of the courage and determination that Henry Winstanley and John Smeaton must have needed to land and build a lighthouse on that terrifying reef.

"There they are," shouted the cox'n, pointing up at the lighthouse.

I peered through the flying spray, and there on the top balcony a tiny figure was waving towards us.

"Stand by for the rope," called the cox'n to the crew. Then he grabbed a loud hailer and his voice boomed out across the sea.

"We're standing by for a line!"

There was another wave from the lighthouse.

"Hold her steady," the cox'n shouted to the helmsman—then through the loud hailer again, "Right—Fire!"

There was a flash and a muffled bang, and then a graceful curve of red sparks cut across the sky. The rocket carrying the rope landed about ten yards from the boat, and in seconds it was grabbed by hooks and hauled aboard.

We were in touch with Eddystone!

The first to go was the turkey, swinging its way along the rope, and up to the top of the lighthouse above the raging sea.

As it disappeared through a haze of spume, I felt glad we'd taken the trouble to put it in a waterproof bag!

Crackers, puddings, paper hats, mail and parcels from home all bobbed their way along the rope and into the hands of the waiting lighthousemen. When the final parcel had been safely landed, the cox'n handed me the loud hailer.

"A Happy Christmas from all of us on Blue Peter," I boomed.

They waved and shouted something back, but we couldn't hear them. At last we gave a final wave and headed back towards the mainland.

It was growing dark when we arrived in Plymouth Harbour. From high up on the Hoe we could see the stab of light flash out from the Eddystone reef.

I turned to Lesley and said,

"I don't really think I'd like to spend Christmas Day out there, do you?"

The beam of light swept across the sea again.

"No, but I'm glad *somebody*'s going to be there," she said. "And at least we know they've got a turkey and a Christmas pud!"

Bengo

THREE STORIES WITHOUT WORDS
by Tim

As far as we know, Mr Ray Cook of Pinner
is the only matchstick mini carver in Britain
—which isn't really so surprising when you
think the average match measures
2 millimetres by 4½ centimetres.

When Mr Cook brought his miniature
carvings to the Blue Peter studio, we had to
fit a special lens to one of our cameras
before we could take pictures of them,
because with the naked eye, it's impossible
to tell how much detail has gone into each
match.

mini MASTERPIECES

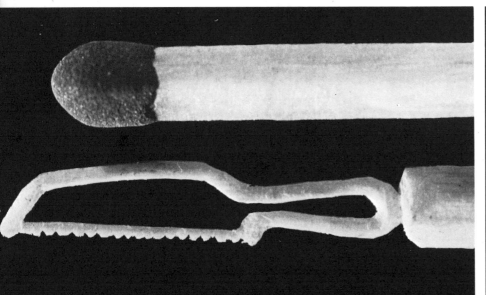

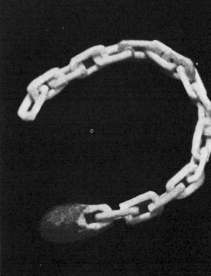

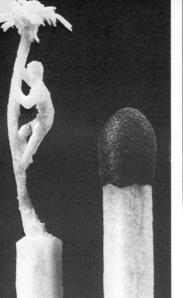

The only tool Mr Cook uses is a piece of razor-blade, broken off to make a point, with some sticky tape round one end so that he doesn't cut himself. With this improvised knife, he transforms matches into anything from ladders, forks and scissors, to a man doing a handstand, a woman with a tiny umbrella, and a whole assortment of animals and acrobats.

By now, of course, Mr Cook is a pretty good judge of a strong matchstick. Although it's such a fiddly job, only about one in ten of his attempts fails because the match actually breaks. The main problem is faulty matches—a great many won't do because they have faults in the grain. Mr Cook told us he can only use five or six at the most out of a box of forty, but only one or two of his carvings are second attempts, for he gets most of them perfect first time.

There are other pitfalls as well—Mr Cook has learnt from bitter experience that some things just don't fit into the shape of a match—things like elephants and tortoises, both of which he's tried and had to throw away.

The carving Mr Cook says is his greatest technical achievement is one of the most simple-looking. It's an 18-link chain and each link took an hour to finish. At the end there's the unlighted head of the match, so the whole thing looks like a ball and chain.

Another carving Mr Cook's particularly proud of is a man climbing a palm tree. He did it as an experiment, and one of the remarkable things about it is that the leaves of the palm tree are spread wider than the width of the matchstick! This technique of spreading the wood is one of the most difficult things Mr Cook's had to learn.

There's something else beside perseverance and patience that's remarkable about Mr Cook. For the last 10 years he's been crippled with rheumatoid arthritis. Both hands are becoming limited in movement and strength, yet Mr Cook is convinced that his hobby helps keep his joints supple. So if any friends of yours have arthritis of the hands, show them these pictures—perhaps they too, will help conquer their arthritis by turning into matchstick mini carvers.

PADDINGTON'S
PUZZLE

A story by Michael Bond
Illustrated by "Hargreaves"

Paddington was at a loose end. Or rather, to be more exact he was at a loose end in the loft of number thirty-two Windsor Gardens; a situation that would have caused a certain amount of alarm among the rest of the household had they been in a position to know about it.

But fortunately for their peace of mind they were elsewhere at that moment, and busy with other things. Mr Brown was at his office; Jonathan and Judy were at school; and with Christmas only a short way away, Mrs Brown and her housekeeper, Mrs Bird, were out for the day doing some "secret" shopping.

It was largely because he'd been left to his own devices that Paddington had eventually ended up in the loft. His own Christmas list was far from complete, and he'd really gone up there in the hope of getting some ideas from all the old things that were stored there.

Paddington was rather keen on the Browns' loft and it wasn't often he had the chance to pay it a visit. Even the act of having to climb a pair of steps and push open the trapdoor was somehow more exciting than going into an ordinary room.

It was the smell he remembered most of all; a musty mixture of mothballs, old clothes, cardboard and dry air, that was really quite pleasant when you got used to it.

The rafters were chock-a-block with bits and pieces; boxes of long-forgotten games, old curtains, toys, rolls of carpet, dolls, and packing cases overflowing with junk of every kind; in fact, there was so much he hardly knew where to start.

In the end he picked on the packing case nearest to him and began unloading it bit by bit. It was a slow job, for the more he took out the more there seemed to be left inside, and he kept coming across things that needed investigating.

He was so busy the time simply melted away, and it wasn't until he came across a large cardboard box with a brightly coloured picture on the lid that he took his first pause for breath.

The picture showed a small boy sitting at a table hard at work with a most unusual-looking saw, and by a strange coincidence it was almost identical to one John had used earlier in the week in a "Blue Peter" item on fretwork. Seeing the picture brought it all back and set Paddington's mind awhirl.

Paddington liked carpentry, but he didn't get much opportunity to do any. Whenever Mrs Bird saw him with tools in his paws she always sent him out into the garden, and the idea of having a carpentry set you were actually *meant* to use indoors seemed a very good idea indeed.

The inside of the box was even more exciting, for it was still full of the original tools – each one mounted in its own specially shaped hole. Admittedly the fretsaw had gone slightly rusty over the years, but there were several unused blades left, not to mention a small drill, some sandpaper, several sheets of plywood, and a selection of paper patterns for good measure.

Paddington came to a decision. His find seemed like a heaven-sent opportunity to kill several birds with one stone. He felt sure that even Mrs Bird couldn't be cross with him if he used the outfit in order to make Christmas presents for the rest of the family, and a few moments later, clutching the box in his paws, he clambered back through the trapdoor and hurried downstairs.

His first port of call was the kitchen, and for the next half-hour all was quiet as he busied himself making up some flour and water paste so that he could stick the various patterns onto the plywood, just as John had shown on the television.

Paddington didn't believe in doing things by halves, and he soon had a bucket overflowing with paste ready for the off.

Shortly afterwards, back in his own room, a steady sound of sawing filled the air as he set to work.

At first sight, even though they'd been well and truly stuck to the plywood, the patterns looked a bit complicated. But remembering some of the tips John had passed on, about always keeping the wood firm and the fretsaw itself upright so that the blade didn't twist and break, everything seemed to go surprisingly well. The nice thing about fretwork seemed to be that you never, ever, followed a straight line when a wiggly one would do, and this suited Paddington down to the ground, because some of his own lines were very wiggly indeed.

The more he did the more pleased he began to feel about the way things were going. In no time at all he'd completed quite a number of items – more even than were shown on the lid of the box. Mr Brown had come off best of all, with no less than three pipe racks; but there was also a trinket box for Mrs Brown, a saucepan-lid holder for Mrs Bird, a tie-rack for Jonathan, and another smaller box for Judy to keep her odds and ends in.

Unfortunately, when he blew the sawdust away he found he'd also made a hole in the top of his dressing table.

Paddington was most upset about the hole, but luckily he managed to find the missing piece, and after busying himself with a pot of glue he soon had it almost back to normal. In fact, after rubbing the spot with some marmalade it was hard to see where it had happened.

It was while he was mending the hole in his dressing table that Paddington suddenly had an idea for what was really one of his most important Christmas presents of all; the one he always sent the "Blue Peter" team.

It was never easy trying to think up presents for all four, and although Paddington was a generous bear at heart he somehow felt it was much better value to send one good one they

could all share rather than several not such good
ones.

Until it had been repaired, the top of his
dressing table had looked not unlike an
unfinished jig-saw puzzle, and a jig-saw puzzle
seemed the ideal answer to his problem.
Paddington was sure that given the right picture
he would be able to make a very good puzzle
indeed.

Many times in the past he'd found that ideas
and good luck often went together – the one
seemingly being triggered off by the other, and it
was while he was gazing out of his window
wondering where on earth he could find a
suitable picture, that the kitchen door belonging
to the house next door suddenly opened and
Mr Curry, the Browns' neighbour, came into
view carrying a large, oblong object in his arms.

Even from as far away as his bedroom window
Paddington could see that it was a picture of
some kind, and his eyes grew larger and larger
as Mr Curry, after hesitating for a moment or
two, propped it against his dustbin and then
went back into his house.

Paddington could hardly believe his good
fortune. Normally he wouldn't have dreamed of
asking the Browns' neighbour for anything.
Apart from having a reputation for being
extremely bad-tempered, Mr Curry was also well
known in the district for his meanness. He rarely,
if ever, threw anything away, so if he put
anything out with the rubbish it was a certainty
he couldn't possibly have any further use for it.

Paddington hurried downstairs and made his
way round the side of the house. In order to
make doubly sure he knocked on Mr Curry's
back door, but there was such a noise going on
inside the house even though he tried several
times there was no reply, so he turned his
attention to the matter in hand.

The picture wasn't the only thing Mr Curry
had put out with his rubbish. Standing beside the
dustbin was a pile of old magazines, an
occasional table, an umbrella stand, and various
other items.

Paddington recognised the picture as one
Mr Curry usually kept hanging in his hall. It
showed a gentleman in frilly clothes and a
fancy hat. He wore a large moustache and a
happy smile on his face, but what pleased
Paddington most of all was the fact that he was
already stuck to a sheet of plywood – just right
for cutting.

Paddington considered the matter for a
moment or two. All in all, he decided that
perhaps it would be better not to bother Mr
Curry again in case it made him change his
mind. Apart from that, he was anxious to begin
work on the jig-saw, and so, after tapping
lightly once more on the door, he picked up the
painting and made his way back home without
waiting to see if the knocks were answered.

Paddington soon decided that cutting out
jig-saw puzzles was much the best use for a
fret-saw. It was even easier than making

pipe-racks. It was really only a matter of moving
the saw up and down as fast as it would go,
turning the wood in different directions at the
same time, and he grew more and more pleased
as one by one the pieces fell to the floor and the
pile at his feet grew higher.

When he got to the end he put them all
carefully into a cardboard box, wrapped the
box itself in some special Christmas paper, and
then spent some time making out a label marked
A PRESENT FOR YOU in large green letters.

As it happened the ink had barely time to dry
when there was a ring at the front door bell, and
thinking perhaps the Browns had arrived home
extra early Paddington hurried downstairs with
the parcel.

To his surprise it wasn't the Browns at all;
it was Mr Curry. He didn't seem in a very good
mood, and for some reason or other he sounded
even more cross when Paddington announced
that he was on his own.

"I'd like to use your phone, bear," he growled,
as he followed Paddington into the hall. "I have
just been robbed of a very valuable item. And I
might say it isn't surprising if everybody goes
out. It's asking for trouble."

While he was talking Mr Curry caught sight
of the box in Paddington's paws, and when he
saw the words on the lid his expression softened.

"Fancy you going to all that trouble just for
me, bear!" he exclaimed, all thoughts of his
telephone call forgotten for the moment.

Paddington stared at him in alarm. "Oh, I
haven't been to any trouble for you, Mr Curry,"
he began. "I *wouldn't* . . . I mean . . ."

Mr Curry held up his hand. "There's no need to say another word, bear," he announced, pushing open the dining-room door. "I shan't wait until Christmas. I shall open it here and now."

Paddington watched gloomily as without further ado Mr Curry tore open the paper and emptied the contents of the box on to the table. Although he always sent the Browns' neighbour a card he didn't normally give him any sort of a present, let alone one he'd made specially for the "Blue Peter" team.

"I'm afraid it's only a jig-saw, Mr Curry," he explained. "I made it with my own paws. If you like," he added hopefully, "I could try and do you something better."

"Nonsense, bear!" said Mr Curry, in an unusually mild tone of voice. "I like jig-saws. I don't know when anyone last gave me one. I must say I'm very touched."

Mr Curry seemed so taken up with the whole affair he began sorting out the pieces straight away. "This is just what I need," he explained. "Something to take my mind off things."

"I've been redecorating my hall," he continued, "and I know you won't believe this, but I stood all the things outside while I was working and someone has stolen a very valuable painting. I left it propped against the dustbin. It could only have been there a few minutes."

Paddington's face grew longer and longer as he listened to Mr Curry.

"I *do* believe you, Mr Curry," he said unhappily as he hurried across the room and began drawing the curtains.

Mr Curry stared after him. "Bear!" he roared, some of his usual bad temper getting the better of him. "What are you doing? I can't see to do my jig-saw!"

"That's good!" exclaimed Paddington. "I . . . I mean . . . " He broke off as he caught sight of the expression on Mr Curry's face, and he began juggling with the folds in the material in the hope of finding a position where the gap let in enough light for the shape of the pieces to be visible without giving away the whole picture.

"My painting," said Mr Curry, placing another piece of puzzle carefully into its correct position, "has been in the family for as long as I can remember. I would go so far as to say it's priceless! Funnily enough, it wasn't unlike . . . "

The Browns' neighbour gave a start as he stared at the half-completed puzzle in front of him.

"Bear!" he bellowed suddenly. "What's the meaning of this? Where are you? Come back here."

But Mr Curry's words fell on stony ground, for Paddington had fled. He felt the moment had definitely come to make himself scarce, and he knew just the place in which to do it.

Although in the course of the day he'd removed quite a few things from the Browns' loft it was still pretty full, and there was certainly more than enough left to make a very good cover for a bear's hideaway.

Paddington felt pleased he'd picked such a good hiding-place. Mr Curry stomped around the house calling out his name for some while, and when he risked a quick peep through the trap-door it gave him quite a shock; for anything less like the happy, smiling face of the man in the jig-saw picture would have been hard to imagine.

But at long last there was a bang and the house shook as the front door slammed shut.

Just to be on the safe side Paddington sat where he was for a moment or two until he felt the coast was clear, and then he crept downstairs. Once there, he made his way in the direction of the telephone; for with Mr Curry in his present mood he had no wish to venture outside. There was no need to look up the number he had in mind, for he'd had occasion to dial it more than once in the past.

Paddington was a great believer in going straight to the top in times of trouble, and he felt sure that if the members of the "Blue Peter" team put their heads together they would be able to think of a way out of his present emergency, especially as it had to do with fretwork and their own Christmas present into the bargain.

*   *   *   *

John gave a cough. "One of the nice things about working on 'Blue Peter', he said, addressing the viewing millions, "is that life is full of surprises."

"Never a dull moment," agreed Peter.

"Who would have thought," continued Lesley, with a straight face, "that when we came into the studio this morning we would end up being the proud owners of a bear's restoration!"

"What's that?" bellowed Mr Curry. He peered at the Browns' television screen as the camera pulled back to reveal an all-too-familiar picture. "That's *my* painting! What's it doing on 'Blue Peter?' Bear! Is this anything to do with you?"

Mr Curry glared round the Browns' dining-room, but if he was hoping for an answer he was disappointed. Paddington was keeping well out of sight, hidden from view by the rest of the family.

The Browns themselves were equally at sea.

They had arrived back from their shopping expedition only to find Mr Curry standing on their front doorstep clutching a telegram bearing the words "IF YOU WATCH BLUE PETER THIS AFTERNOON YOU MAY SEE SOMETHING TO YOUR ADVANTAGE. VAL, JOHN, PETER AND LESLEY". But beyond that they had no knowledge of what had been going on that day. Only Mrs Bird had a nasty feeling it might have something to do with Paddington and Mr Curry's latest outburst confirmed her worst suspicions.

"If you sit still and listen for a moment," she said severely, "perhaps we shall *all* find out what's going on!"

"This painting," said John, as Mr Curry sank back muttering into his chair, "came into our hands just before the programme went on the air."

"You might think," said Peter, running his fingers over the surface, "that it's a priceless work of art."

"Hear! Hear!" murmured Mr Curry, glancing triumphantly at the others. "I'm glad someone's talking sense at last."

"If you thought that," said Lesley, "you would be quite wrong. It's a copy of a very famous painting called *The Laughing Cavalier*, and it's certainly priceless in one meaning of the word – you can practically buy them two a penny."

"Oh, I wouldn't say that," broke in John. "*Three* a penny is more like it. You see them all over the place. In fact, just to prove it we went out and bought some more."

While he was speaking the camera pulled back still further and Valerie came into view standing beside a whole row of identical paintings. She crossed towards Mr Curry's painting and with a single deft movement placed it on a nearby table, removing it from the frame at the same time.

"What makes this one different from the others," she said, "is that it's really two-in-one. You can either have it hanging up . . . "

"Or," said John, as he joined her and broke off one of the corners and held it up to the camera, "you can use it as a jig-saw."

"Just the thing for the long winter evenings," broke in Lesley.

"But what makes it even more interesting," said Peter, as a closer shot of Mr Curry's painting filled the screen, "is that when it's used as a picture it looks exactly like the real thing. The saw-cuts are just like the sort of cracks you get in the paint on a genuine old master."

"In fact," said Valerie, "we're so pleased with our present we are going to hang it in a place of honour in the 'Blue Peter' office. And so that its original owner won't feel too deprived we're sending him one of the other paintings."

"In a spanking new frame," said John. "Which in itself," he added meaningfully, "is worth more than the old one *and* its picture put together."

"So we hope everyone will be happy," concluded Peter. "*We* certainly are. We have a new picture for the office . . . "

"Plus the fun of doing a jig-saw," added Lesley.

"The taxi-driver got an unexpected fare when I went to collect it," continued John.

"The Producers had an item for today's programme," said Valerie, "and last but not least I expect a good many viewers will have got some ideas for their own Christmas presents as well."

"Perhaps, Mr Curry," said Paddington hopefully, as he emerged from behind the sofa, "when your new painting comes I could turn that into a jig-saw as well!"

But his offer fell on deaf ears. The Browns' neighbour was already on his way. And if the expression on his face was anything to go by the answer to Paddington's offer was most definitely "no". Mr Curry looked as if he'd had quite enough of bear's jig-saw puzzles for the time being.

As it was he missed John's closing remark after he'd announced that they would be sending the remaining paintings to Paddington that very afternoon. It was a remark that caused a loud groan to go up not only from Peter, Val and Lesley, but the Browns as well, and one which, had he still been there, Mr Curry would have agreed with to the full.

"After all," said John, "Paddington might want to do some more fretwork and I'd hate to think of him going next-door for another picture. *That* would be the unkindest saw-cut of all!"

Colour the spaces as indicated by the numbers and the mystery picture will appear.

1. Red
2. Light Blue
3. Black
4. Dark Green
5. Light Green
6. Dark Blue
7. Yellow
8. Dark Brown
9. Light Brown

WILDLIFE RESCUE

We said at the beginning of this book that you never know what's going to happen next on Blue Peter. When the telephone rings, it could be someone saying "Come to Tonga", or "Come and airlift a Triceratops to the Isle of Wight".

A call I had a few months ago started off sounding quite normal. It was from naturalist Grahame Dangerfield, and he asked me to meet him, not in the depths of the countryside, but in his home in Hertfordshire. Grahame has quite a collection of animals—not a zoo, because his garden's not open to visitors—but a Wildlife Breeding Centre where he tries to breed rare creatures and help prevent them becoming extinct. The birds and animals live in huge aviaries and enclosures, so you can guess how surprised I was when Grahame showed me into his kitchen. At first, all I could see were pots and pans—

"It's over here," said Grahame. "Something quite new," and he pointed at what looked like a box full of reeds.

I still couldn't see what he was getting at, and then, very suddenly, there was a movement—then another—and another. The box of reeds was alive! It was the home of a group of five harvest mice—Britain's second smallest animal—and according to Grahame they were very rare indeed.

The thought of mice being rare struck me as rather odd. After all, people put down traps and poison to get *rid* of mice in their houses.

But harvest mice are quite different from Mus musculus—that's the house mouse. Normally they live out in the fields amongst the corn and wheat, and in the olden days when farmers cut the corn with scythes, they'd be seen scampering about amongst the sheaves and stubble which was how they came to be called "harvest" mice. But with the modernisation of agricultural methods, farmers cut their corn with combine harvesters. And these huge machines scoop up whole families at once—the nests of babies, mothers and fathers—all with no chance of escape. And this has been happening for so long that harvest mice are seldom seen in the fields nowadays.

Although they're so small—about 5 cms without their tails—there are all kinds of ways in which harvest mice are out of the ordinary. For one thing, they're the only British mammal that lives almost permanently off the ground—although they go down sometimes to feed, they spend most of their lives on the stems of corn. That means they're amazingly nimble and expert at balancing. Grahame told me how they've completely adapted their bodies for climbing, and actually use their tail as a fifth leg. They wrap it round everything to keep their balance and stop themselves falling down. Sometimes they even hang by their tails in mid-air!

This box of reeds in Grahame's kitchen was the home of five harvest mice.

Their nest was superbly camouflaged. When it was first built, it had been perfectly round.

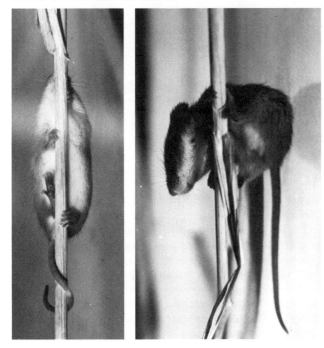

Harvest mice are expert at balancing. They've completely adapted their bodies for climbing, and actually use their tail as a fifth leg. They wrap it round everything to stop themselves falling down, and sometimes even hang by their tails in mid-air.

Inside Grahame's box of reeds, the harvest mouse nest was superbly camouflaged. I could only just see it in the middle, about 60 cm. off the ground. It was looking a bit tatty and pulled about, but Grahame said when it was first built it had been perfectly round with a tiny entrance hole in one side.

The mice certainly seemed very much at home in their box. There were two large perforated zinc grills in the top, which gave them plenty of air, and at the bottom there was a small door so that food could be put inside. I thought that opening the door would be risky, because the mice moved like quicksilver, but Grahame said the noise made them dart upwards, instead of down towards the door, and that so far there'd been no escapes.

Grahame's harvest mouse diet consisted of small pots of corn and mixed seeds and water. The only missing element was insects, which were not always easy to get hold of.

By now the mice were very lively indeed. They didn't seem at all put off by the glass sides of the box, or the sight of Grahame and me peering in at them. That was the whole point of having them in the kitchen. Grahame wanted them to become perfectly used to human beings, and after observing their behaviour in great detail, he'd gradually improve the conditions the mice were living in, until he hoped they became so perfect that the mice would breed.

That was why he'd gone to so much trouble to see that conditions in the box matched harvest mouse life in the fields as closely as possible.

Another reason for keeping the mice in the kitchen, where the light was switched on for about 14 hours each day, was to get them used to artificial light—the idea being they'd be encouraged to breed all the year round, and not just in the late summer.

It seemed to me that the mice were more closely confined than they would have been out of doors, and Grahame said he'd noticed there had been a few fights over "territory". With two males and three females living in a fairly small space, it might be better to leave one pair in the nest and build another box for the others.

But shortage of space or not, three weeks later there was some very good news indeed. Two of the females had babies—nine altogether—and a few weeks later, they had another eleven! Grahame thinks that these are only the third lot of harvest mice born in captivity in Britain, and he hopes that with the adults separated into different cages, he'll be able to breed many more.

But mice in the kitchen weren't Grahame's only surprise—he had foxes in his garage!

Fennec foxes

They were Fennec foxes, said by many people to be the most beautiful animals in the world. I'll never forget the sight of the row of five pairs of pricked ears, and five pairs of round eyes staring at us, as Grahame and I stood in front of them, and five noses quivering as they caught our scent.

Although their faces were fox-shaped, they were really more the size of toy dogs than our British foxes. Their creamy, sandy colour gave a clue about the part of the world they came from—the desert—and I could easily imagine how they'd scarcely be visible against soft, pale sand. Their ears were enormous—no one's really sure why, but the answer could be that they need to have super-sensitive hearing for hunting, or they could be like the elephant which has huge ears to get rid of body heat in a hot climate.

In the wild, Fennec foxes are said to live in groups—unlike the British fox which lives singly or in pairs—and I wondered how on earth they survived in barren deserts. Grahame said they hunted small rodents—things like desert rats, and lots of insects, including locusts. They were also supposed to eat different fruits, which was how they were believed to get their moisture. It's thought they don't drink in the wild.

Grahame said Fennec foxes were found throughout Libya and the desert parts of North Africa. Two of his were males, and three females. Three had come from London Zoo, and two of those were actually born there—Britain's first Fennec fox births. The other two had come from a private collection.

Like the harvest mice, Grahame hoped the foxes would breed—and again that meant giving them the best possible living conditions. The reason for keeping them in the garage loft was very ingenious. Grahame's scheme was to keep out all British daylight—but the foxes didn't live in darkness. A light controlled by a time switch gave them exact Libyan daylight hours, down to the last second. He told me it was a copy of what London Zoo had done, and the Zoo were convinced they'd only been able to breed their two foxes because they had special lighting.

With a collection of five, I thought Grahame's breeding chances were high. But he wasn't so sure. He pointed out one fox sitting apart from the others.

"The male sitting up there on his own is really our only hope of breeding. He's the one that came from the private collection, but unfortunately, he takes very little interest in those two females in the corner. They're sisters that were born at London Zoo, and we hoped he would breed with them because they're nice and young. But they seem to keep to themselves. Then over in the other corner we've got the old grumpy female who ought to have bred by now but hasn't, and she's a bit of a misery—she's the one who would happily bite you. Down below we've got the very old man who's really just come here to retire—he's almost certainly not going to breed. He's very old but he's still quite well."

All the time Grahame was speaking, the foxes were making a low, growling sound. I wondered whether they'd take a flying leap at us, but Grahame said we were quite safe—as long as we didn't get too close! They had extremely sharp teeth and Grahame used thick gloves if he ever had to handle them, which added to the difficulties of looking after them.

I hope Grahame has as much luck with the Fennec foxes as he's had with his harvest mice. He certainly deserves to. It's thanks to dedicated naturalists like him that we're able to learn more about rare and unusual animals and birds.

This wingless wonder is the fastest vehicle I've built. The chassis is made from a balsa wood off-cut, and a propeller and wheels salvaged from broken plastic kits. The electric motor comes from a model shop, but even so my Landflyer works out a lot cheaper than a comparable ready-made. Here are the working drawings and all the instructions:

ELECTRIC LANDFLYER

1 The chassis is cut from a piece of balsa wood 20 cm long, 8 cm wide and 1 cm thick. Measure and mark the shape before you cut.

2 Fix 4 small plastic wheels. Use bead-headed pins for axles and a small bead for a bearing. Because of the pins, you should keep your Landflyer away from small children.

3 The power unit is built up from a 4½-volt battery, 2 empty matchboxes and a 3-volt electric motor. For neatness, I cover the boxes and battery with sticky-backed plastic. Fix all three together with a strong elastic band, then fasten a paper clip to each lead to make the terminal connections.

4 To fit the propeller on to the motor, you may need to enlarge the hole in the propeller box. To do this, put a headless nail in a hand drill and bore through the propeller. It is a good idea to place the propeller on a bit of cut-off balsa wood and get someone to hold it steady while you are drilling.

5 Push the pointed end of the propeller boss on to the motor shaft. It is important to put it this way round because it is at the back of the Landflyer, pushing and not pulling.

6 Fix the power unit to the chassis with another strong elastic band. Connect the leads from the engine to the battery with the paper clips. If your Landflyer shoots off backwards, change the clips round. You should be off to a flying start!

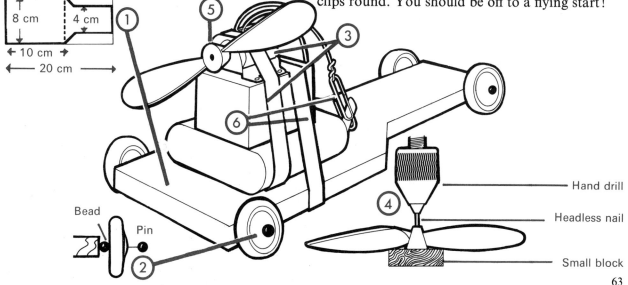

SKYLAB

Following the successful missions to the Moon, comes the launching of Skylab, the next step in man's exploration of Space.

Skylab is America's first manned Space Station and is a completely self-contained living and workshop unit. Its object is to provide information on how men can live and work for long periods in Space, as well as providing an observation post for viewing both the Sun and Earth.

As it circles Earth at a height of some 235 miles Skylab will be visited by three-man crews who will stay on board for periods of 28 and 56 days, returning to Earth by the splash-down method which successfully rounded off the Moon shots.

Geoffrey WHEELER

Dining at the wardroom table. Prepacked food is heated in the overhead "cooker".

The enormous Saturn V launch vehicle used to hoist Skylab into Space. The Apollo module containing crew members is launched separately by a smaller Saturn 1B.

Sleeping— bat fashion! In Space a crewman is not aware of being upside-down. Snug in his sleeping bag slung between the lattice "floor" and "ceiling" the sleeper may be constantly checked by instruments through a special "night-cap," to see how well he sleeps.

Cycling in Space. A crewman uses the Bicycle Ergometer, a means of getting daily exercise at the same time checking his energy output.

(1) Skylab's Living Space. Here the crew members live, eat and sleep — and take their exercise.
(2) Wardroom, with its dining-table, cooker and food storage cupboards. One luxury — a window looking out on Earth.
(3) Sleeping Compartment, divided into small cubicles in which the men sling their sleeping bags and sleep suspended between "floor" and "ceiling".
(4) Waste Management Compartment containing washing facilities and lavatory.
(5) Refuse Disposal Unit.
(6) Workshop Area, where experiments are carried out.

(7) Centre pole along which crew men steer themselves as they "float from one compartment to another.
(8) Food storage cupboards. Enough food is carried for three separate visits of three-man crews, the first visit lasting 28 days; the second and third for 56 days each.
(9) Food freezers.
(10) Water storage tanks.
(11) Air bottles containing oxygen and nitrogen.
(12) Apollo three-man spacecraft specially adapted from the Moon-shot craft to transport the three-man crew to and from Skylab.
(13) Additional docking port to accept a second Apollo spacecraft should a rescue be necessary.

(14) Airlock Module which seals off the Skylab from Apollo. This allows crewmen to discard their space suits and live inside Skylab in lightweight overalls.
(15) Solar Telescope.
(16) Solar batteries providing electricity for the Solar Telescope.
(17) Walking — and working — in Space, to replace the Solar Telescope cartridges.
(18) Solar batteries providing electricity for the main compartments.

Skylab

UNITED STATES

USA

Weight (at launching) 197,000 lbs; Length, including Apollo 118.5 ft.; Diameter of living space cylinder 21.6 ft.

LITTLE ANGELS

The day we had a studio full of Angels is one we'll never forget! These thirty 8- to 15-year-olds from Korea have been called the most famous children's ballet in the world, and when you look at their list of achievements, that's not at all surprising. After all, there can't be many children who've met The Queen, two United States Presidents, three Prime Ministers, and dozens of princes and princesses. During their six world tours, the Little Angels have given over 600 performances in front of 720,000 people, and to do this, they've travelled 284,000 miles by bus and plane.

Miss Hong Eee Lee was one of the eight Little
Angels who performed the Penitent Monks' Drum
dance. It's supposed to symbolise the monks'
struggle between good and evil, and each girl
beats a set of six drums.

At the end of the dance, I was given a lesson by
Miss Hi Young Suh. The movements were
incredibly fast and complicated, and quite unlike
anything I'd done with the Young Generation!

The five musicians were members of the National
Court Music Academy. Between them they
played more than 50 unusual instruments
including an hourglass-shaped drum.

This line-up of Little Angels includes their
founder, Colonel Bo Hi Pak. Some of the girls are
wearing their smart blue and white travelling
outfits.

At home in Korea Miss Jung
Lim Cho and Miss Sung Lim
Lee set off for school. For
their ordinary lessons the
Little Angels wear school
uniform and their classes
are arranged just like ours in
Britain. Some children join
the company as young as
four years old and the limit
is fifteen. When they
"retire" most Little Angels
become teachers or dancers
with other groups.

I was given a lesson in using chopsticks when I was invited to join the Little Angels for a Korean meal, backstage at Sadler's Wells Theatre.

My attempts weren't very good—but the food was delicious—soup, a mixture of meat and mushrooms, rice, seaweed and a special kind of omelette!

The children help each other with their make-up. The eyes and cheeks are coloured first—then they put on their lipstick, and last of all they arrange their hair. Their pink blouses are called Chokoris and their long skirts are Chimas.

This tea party gave the Little Angels a chance to try out Western food. They were the guests of Blue Peter viewers Stephen, Daniel, Julie and Joanne Alston. The twins, Julie and Joanne, came from Korea themselves and were adopted by the Alstons when they were four years old.

Wherever they go, the Little Angels are showered with compliments and applause—all fully deserved because their dancing is breathtakingly good—but is it possible to receive such continuous praise and attention and not become unpleasantly big-headed?

The answer is "Yes". We'd never met such polite and thoughtful visitors, and even though we could hardly speak a word of each other's languages, we felt the Little Angels welcomed *us*, just as much as we were enjoying seeing them. During rehearsals they were far more professional than members of many adult companies, and when we discovered how difficult it was to become a Little Angel, and how tough the training was, we began to understand how they had achieved such a high reputation.

Strangely enough, the company was founded not by a ballerina, but by a Colonel in the Korean Army.

Colonel Bo Hi Pak was sickened by the destruction and suffering he saw during the terrible Korean war. Peace came, and although

Korea was devastated, the Colonel thought there was still something good his country could give to the world. Korea is rich in dancing and music. Some of the traditional dances are over 2000 years old, and they're full of legends and folklore.

In 1962, Colonel Bo Hi Pak hunted high and low for the very best dancers—he wanted children, not grown-ups, because he thought children would symbolise the spirit of the new Korea that had risen out of the terrible war.

Dance competitions were held and there were hundreds and hundreds of auditions. Only the very best were chosen, and then the children were given three years' rigorous training before they were allowed to appear in public.

When they did, the effect was electrifying. Never before had people seen such young dancers give such amazing performances.

For children to have achieved such world-wide success is truly incredible—that's why millions of people—not only us—will never forget the Little Angels of Korea.

GARDEN GLAMOUR

Let your doll relax in a luxury swing hammock in her own beautiful garden. A shoe-box and two wire coat-hangers can be converted into a comfortable seat, and with some ceiling tiles you can make lawns, rose beds and even an ornamental pond.

1 The frame for the swing hammock is made from two stiff wire coat-hangers. Cut the hooks off and straighten the wire outwards into the frame shape.
Keep the little curved bits at the end because they make good feet. By winding white sticky tape round the frame you can fasten the two hangers together and give them a smart finish at the same time.

2 The seat is made from a shoe-box. Cut one side off at a slope, then paint it, or cover it with sticky-backed plastic.
Thread two pieces of white string through little holes in the box and fasten them with a knot. This makes the white ropes for the seat to swing on.
When you're satisfied that the seat is hanging straight and even, fasten the ropes in place on the frame with a little piece of sticky tape.

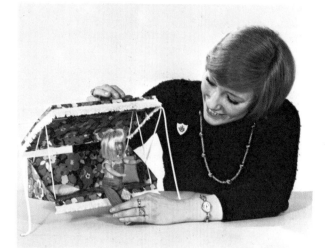

3 Cover the shoe-box lid to match the seat and make a shady canopy.
Cut two slots about a third of the way along the short sides of the box so that it will slip over the top bar of the frame. Then fasten it firmly to the bar with sticky tape.

4 White fringe trimming glued round the seat and the canopy gives the swing hammock a very glamorous look.
You can make little cushions from scraps of material, too, so that your doll can lie back in luxury and enjoy her garden.

5 Patterned ceiling tiles are ideal for the garden because, painted with grey emulsion or poster paint, they look just like crazy paving. The separate pieces cut out easily too, so you can use them to make rockeries or walls.
For grass you can paint the plain side of the tile green, or cover them with green material if you happen to have some.

6 With three tiles you can make a pond with real water. Take the middle out of two tiles and make a smaller hole in the top tile. Glue all three together with the one with the small hole on top. Make sure to use a white glue—other kinds dissolve the polystyrene. Paint the surround grey, and then slip a small plate or saucer underneath to hold the water.

7 For a realistic look, glue the spare pieces round the pond to make a little rockery wall. It's easy to make plants, too, by folding coloured paper tissue into flower shapes. When they're glued on to cocktail sticks, or spent matches, they can be "planted" straight into the ceiling tiles.

8 With the left-over pieces of tile, all sorts of things can be made for the garden. Little bits of foam plastic stuck on to real twigs make good trees. These can be planted in plasticine, pressed into a piece of tile with a wall round to give a nice finish. I wonder what ideas you'll have for your garden?

RAHERE The Story of 'Barts'

This is "Barts"–Saint Bartholomew's Hospital, right in the busy heart of London. These buildings are 250 years old, but there has been a hospital here caring for the sick and the aged and homeless for more than 800 years. And the man who founded Barts so many centuries ago still lies in his magnificent tomb in the church of St Bartholomew the Great next door. His name was Rahere and it's said he was a minstrel at the Court of King Henry I.

Rahere sang songs, told stories, and made jokes. His job was to provide the entertainment for the court, and although he came from a poor family, all the courtiers knew him, and even the King himself and the Prince laughed at his jokes. Then one day a sad thing happened. The young Prince made a journey to France on a boat, called the White Ship. During the crossing there was a great storm, the White Ship sank, and the young Prince was drowned.

The King was horrified—it is said he never smiled again. The gay court of Henry I was plunged into sadness and Rahere began to wonder whether there was more to life than entertaining courtiers.

The next day, he asked the King's permission to go on a pilgrimage to Rome, and he dressed in the simple clothes of a poor pilgrim. In Rome, Rahere wandered by the marshy banks of the river Tiber, thinking things over. But he caught a kind of fever, probably malaria, and became very ill. He was looked after by some monks, who had founded a hospital in Rome and given up their lives to care for sick pilgrims. And Rahere declared that if he got better, he would go back to London and start a hospital there. As he tossed deliriously in fever, half unconscious and desperately ill, he had a dream— a kind of vision.

"I am Bartholomew", the figure said. "Go back to London, build your hospital and a church in Smithfield. Name them after me, and I will watch over them." Vision or dream, Rahere saw this as the clear plan he was looking for.

He *did* get well and as he recovered, he talked to the kind monks about their hospital, and made ready for his journey home.

Back in London, Rahere became a monk himself—and dressed in a white robe with a black cloak and hood. Together with the Bishop of London, who became his friend, he went once more to see Henry, the King. Not to tell jokes now, but to tell him what his plans were—and Henry gave him authority to go ahead.

Rahere went to Smithfield. A horse-market was held there every Friday, so it was a busy crowded place. People looked curiously at the tall monk surrounded by masons and builders holding plans. Quickly, Rahere turned to the crowd, and talked as he used to tell stories to the court. He told them about his plans for the hospital, and asked them to help.

"If you can't give money, come and work on the site for a few hours," he appealed.

Building started, and slowly the walls began to rise. Rahere planned to build not only a hospital for the sick and aged and homeless, but a monastery for the monks and nursing sisters who would look after them, and a Priory Church where everyone could worship. All were to be dedicated to St Bartholomew, and this was in the year 1123.

Patients began to arrive long before the building was finished and the name of the first patient, written in a great record book, was "Adwyn of Dunwich". Then King Henry himself came to St Bartholomew's and saw the long wards full of patients, looked after by the monks and the sisters.

He saw the beautiful church, with its rounded arches, too, and here the King declared Rahere was the first Master of the Hospital and Prior of

the Monastery, and that the hospital and its patients were under the King's special protection.

Rahere was truly thankful. He had completed the work he had to do—the court minstrel had founded London's greatest hospital!

And 850 years later, Barts remembers its founder in many different ways. The hospital's writing paper, for instance, bears the words: *Telegraphic Address: "Rahere", Cent. London.*

NURSE LESLEY JUDD

I became so interested in St Bartholomew's Hospital, I decided to try and find out what it is like training as a nurse there. I was allowed to join the other trainees and go round the wards with them, and I discovered that an ex-dancer and a nurse have quite a lot in common!

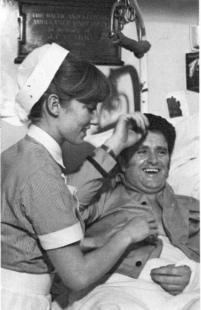

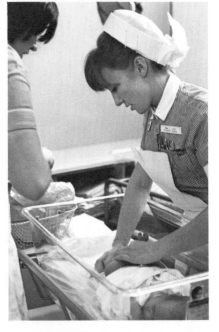

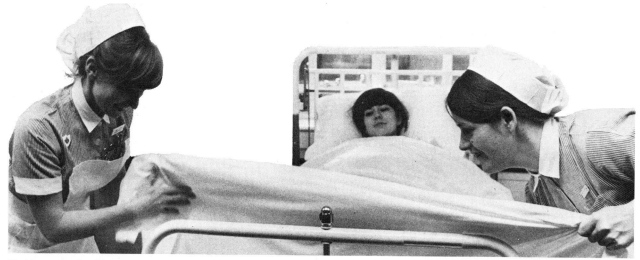

Making a bed with someone in it isn't all that easy, especially if that someone is seriously ill and mustn't be disturbed

I had to call Lynne Nurse Glasson when we were on the wards

The new shift is briefed by the Ward Sister

To start with, they both work long, hard hours—mostly on their feet! And it's mainly women who give the orders in both professions. But the strongest similarity is the comradeship. I had the same feeling of "all in it together" in the nurses' rest room, as I had in the big dancers' dressing-room when I was in the Young Generation.

I must admit that I very much enjoyed wearing the uniform. It's neat and practical – and I don't think any girl can avoid looking pretty in it!

I didn't go straight on the wards to begin with, but I joined a class of student nurses who were being taught how to make beds. A nurse spends a lot of her time making beds, and like everything else on the wards, it's done by a set method. Making a bed with someone in it isn't all that easy—especially if that someone is seriously ill and mustn't be disturbed. We practised with one of the students "lying in" for a patient. I learnt how to make hospital corners which is very satisfying once you get the trick of it, and how to change the bottom sheet with a patient who can't be moved.

I was put with Lynne Glasson, a fully trained nurse, who was responsible for showing me what to do. She's a nice girl of about my age, and we got on very well together. After the bed-making lesson, I turned to her and said:

"Lynne, when we go on the ward . . . "

"The first thing you must do is stop calling me Lynne," she said.

"Why?" I asked, a little taken aback.

"I don't mean all the time," she smiled, "but it isn't allowed on the wards—you must call me Nurse Glasson, and I'll call you Nurse Judd, O.K.?"

I didn't feel that I was good enough to be called "Nurse" yet, but I fell in behind Nurse Glasson and followed her down a series of endless corridors towards "Henry". Henry was not (as I thought at first) the name of a patient, but the name of the Men's Orthopaedic Ward. An orthopaedic ward, I was told, is mostly people with broken bones. On the way, Lynne explained why we had to call each other "Nurse" when we were on the wards.

"It's for the patients, really. It makes them feel much more secure to hear Nurse Glasson's

Under Nurse Glasson's direction, I helped to give Mr Dixon a wash—he had multiple fractures and couldn't move without difficulty. Washing someone with broken arms and fingers, *and* taking care not to wet the sheets, is really quite tricky

Nurse Glasson showed me the tablets for Mr Macdonald

We checked that everyone on the ward had been given the correct medicines

pouring out their medicine, rather than just a girl called Lynne."

We arrived on the ward and reported to Sister Clemens. The other nurses on the shift had just arrived and we all sat round sister's desk to be briefed. This was an up-to-date report on every patient in the ward and the allocation of special duties to individual nurses.

"Mr Jackson's making satisfactory progress and can move his fingers a little, but he must be encouraged to exercise them."

The sisters wear a different uniform from the nurses which has a belt with a silver buckle. They've had years of experience and have passed the State Registered Nurse's examination. Sister is completely in charge of the ward. Her word is law to the nurses, the patients, and occasionally to some of the Junior doctors!

"Nurse Glasson, will you take Nurse Judd and go and wash Mr Dixon."

Mr Dixon had multiple fractures from an accident on a building site, and could do little for himself.

"Hello, Mr Dixon, we've come to give you a wash," smiled Lynne briskly. "You don't mind

if I show Nurse Judd what to do?"

Mr Dixon kindly allowed me to wash his hands and face whilst Lynne directed the operation. Washing someone with broken arms and broken fingers, *and* taking care not to wet the sheets, is really quite tricky.

Lynne told me that when people come in from an accident all dirty and covered with blood, it gives her tremendous satisfaction to get them clean and changed, and tucked up beneath gleaming sheets with immaculate hospital corners.

Next to Mr Dixon was Mr Macdonald who had to have two pain-killing tablets every four hours. Lynne took the appropriate tablets from the medicine chest and handed them to Mr Macdonald, while I entered the time and the dose on a chart at the bottom of his bed.

"What's next, Nurse Glasson?" I asked.

"I think we'll go and have a look at the Maternity Ward," she said.

There's no need to ask the way to the Maternity Ward—just follow the sound of the yells and you'll get there. Human beings are born with three basic instincts, to feed, to sleep

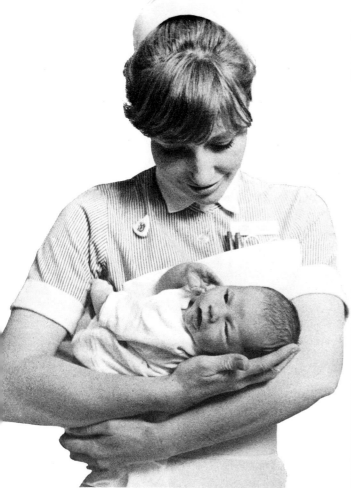

The next call was the maternity ward where I met baby Jason

I successfully changed his nappy and slipped him back into the cot

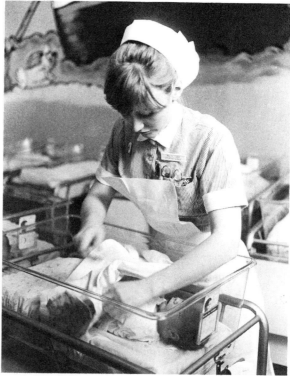

and to cry, and they do all three with matchless concentration.

Having a baby is absolutely exhausting. The very next day the mother has to feed it every three or four hours round the clock! It's no wonder that the mothers look forward to the afternoons, because at Barts the babies are taken away into the nursery whilst their mothers catch up on some sleep!

But it's not an hour off for the nurses. I was in charge of Mrs Collins's son called Jason. The cots are all on wheels, so I pushed baby Jason through into the nursery to join the others. It was quite quiet to begin with, and then one of the babies started to whimper very softly. The one in the cot next door began to join in, and within seconds every baby in the nursery was yelling its head off. The noise was really incredible, but Lynne and the others hardly seemed to notice as they began deftly and methodically to change the nappies.

I started on baby Jason, who by now was red with fury, and flailing his arms and legs all over the place. This was very different from washing a prone and helpless adult. Under Lynne's instructions, I carefully changed Jason's nappy, and then waited for further orders.

"Pick him up and tuck him under your right arm," shouted Lynne above the bellowing. The effect was marvellous. Jason suddenly stopped yelling as if he'd been turned off at the mains. I slipped him back into his cot and immediately he closed his eyes and went fast asleep. I made my way back to the ward.

"Mrs Collins, I've changed baby Jason and he's settling down nicely."

She smiled up at me sleepily.

"Thank you, nurse," she said.

For a moment I felt as though I really belonged.

The companionship in the Nurses' Rest Room reminded me of life in a dancer's dressing-room.

Solutions

PUZZLE PICTURES

1 Val climbed 17 feet down this manhole in York to explore the network of newly discovered **Roman Sewers.**

2 This **Jabberwock** was part of a special Lewis Carroll exhibition held at Longleat.

3 **David Cassidy** helped to judge the 152,200 entries for our Blue Peter "Keep Britain Tidy" Poster competition.

4 The **Vigintipede**—the world's longest tandem bicycle—steered by comedian Ronnie Barker.

5 Learning how to sail a boat without leaving dry land on a very unusual machine.

6 Removing the bell from the front of the **Flying Scotsman** after her American tour.

7 This model **Eiffel Tower** made by Corporal Arthur Riley of Sheffield contains 30,765 matches.

8 **Wamp Wan, M.B.E.**—a stone age tribal Chief from New Guinea.

9 Flag waving by the **Boerk Naas Flag Wavers** from St Nicholas in Belgium.

10 The children of Class 6 of the Sacred Heart Junior School at Teddington made this painting which is a hundred and fifty-five metres long.

11 An acrobatic cook from the **Mansudai National Dance Company of the Democratic People's Republic of Korea.**

THE CASE OF THE MISSING LINK

1 Blue Peter is transmitted "live" on Mondays and Thursdays, therefore the electrician couldn't have worked on the programme on a Wednesday.

2 No one knew of the President's arrival in a mini van except McCann, Bob, the President and Duffinger. Therefore, Duffinger and the electrician must have been involved in a plot.

3 Lamps are not measured in volts, but in watts, as any electrician would know.

4 The electrician could not have broken his watch working in the Diorama studio in the morning as he had already said he did not arrive until after lunch.

5 Television studio cameras are electronic. It is impossible to load them with film as anyone working in the studio would know.

Useful Information

Blue Peter Mini Books
Book of Television
Book of Teddy's Clothes
Book of Pets
Safari to Morocco
Expedition to Ceylon
Book of Presents
Book of Daniel
Book of Guide Dogs
Blue Peter Royal Safari
Blue Peter Book of Limericks
Blue Peter Special Assignment
    London, Amsterdam & Edinburgh
Blue Peter Special Assignment
    Rome, Paris & Vienna

Isle of Wight Monsters,
Blackgang, Isle of Wight.
Crystal Palace Monsters,
Crystal Palace Park, S.E.19.
Corbridge Roman Station,
Corbridge, Northumberland.
Housesteads Roman Fort,
Housesteads, Haydons Bridge, Northumberland.
York Archaeological Trust,
47 Aldwark, York.
Hackney Speedway,
Hackney Stadium, Waterden Road, E.15.
Nursing & Hospital Careers Information Office, 121 Edgware Road, W.1.
Thatching Information:
CoSira, 35 Camp Road, S.W.19.
Tonga Tourist Board,
New Zealand House, Haymarket, S.W.1.
Shetland Tourist Organisation,
Alexandra Wharf, Lerwick, Shetland.

Acknowledgements

"The Cornish Adventure" and "Roman Reporter" were written by Dorothy Smith; the illustrations for *The Eddystone Light* and *Rahere* were by Robert Broomfield; *Bleep & Booster, Bengo* and the *Mystery Picture* by "Tim"; *The Case of the Missing Link* was illustrated by Bernard Blatch; *Roman Reporter* illustrations by Mark Peppé; *Sky Lab* by Geoffrey Wheeler.

Photographs in this book were taken by:
Joan Williams, Charles Walls, Barry Boxall, Dennis Waugh, Bob Loosemore, J. Allan Cash, Camera Press, Daily Express, Radio Times Hulton Picture Library, Picturepoint, John Adcock, Douglas Bentley, Dennis Cartwright, Michael Cook, Peter Edwards, Rosemary Gill, Malcolm Hill, Ken Looms, Franco Martinez & Mike Spooner.

BIDDY BAXTER, EDWARD BARNES & ROSEMARY GILL WOULD LIKE TO ACKNOWLEDGE THE HELP OF GILLIAN FARNSWORTH & MARGARET PARNELL

Cover & book designed by John Strange

Blue Peter

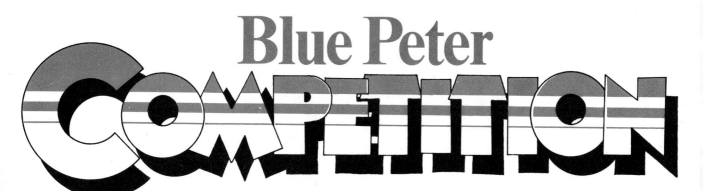

COMPETITION

Would you like to meet Valerie, John, Peter, Lesley and the rest of the Blue Peter team? Would you like to see all the animals? Would you like to come to London and have tea with them all? This is your chance!

The First Prize will be an invitation to an exciting

Blue Peter Party

and there will be lots of competition badges for the runners-up, too.

At Christmas the Blue Peter studio was crammed with decorations. Our ship was there as usual—but where was it? Mark a cross on the picture to show where you think it was.

Cut out your entry
and send it to:
**Blue Peter Competition,
BBC Television Centre,
London W12 7RJ**

Name _____ Age _____

Address _____

First Prize winners and runners-up will be notified by letter. The closing date for entries is 10th January 1974.